'You should ... **he said.**

'What?'

'Smile.' Esteban leaned forward and touched one corner of her mouth. 'It looks good on you. Like a girl coming out to play after too long.'

Nicky felt as if the floor had given way under her. From relief she went to black panic. She thought, This is a game to him.

'All I did was say you are attractive.'

She swallowed. 'What makes you think I want to be attractive?'

Esteban stroked one finger along the line of her tense jaw. The movement was very gentle, very slow. It was hardly a touch at all. And totally intimate.

'You suspect I'm interested in you,' he said calmly. 'And you don't know how to handle it. You're right.' His voice was a purr. 'I am interested.' His eyes travelled over her like a caress. 'The point is, are you?'

Born in London, **Sophie Weston** is a traveller by nature who started writing when she was five. She wrote her first romance recovering from illness, thinking her travelling was over. She was wrong, but she enjoyed it so much that she has carried on. These days she lives in the heart of the city with two demanding cats and a cherry tree—and travels the world looking for settings for her stories.

Recent titles by the same author:

THE MILLIONAIRE AFFAIR

THE LATIN AFFAIR

BY
SOPHIE WESTON

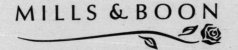

MILLS & BOON

First published in Great Britain 1999
Harlequin Mills & Boon Limited,
Eton House, 18-24 Paradise Road, Richmond, Surrey TW9 1SR

© Sophie Weston 1999

ISBN 0 263 81910 8

Set in Times Roman 10 on 11 pt.
02-0001-54346 C1

Printed and bound in Spain
by Litografia Rosés, S.A., Barcelona

PROLOGUE

'YOU'RE a fraud, Nicky.'

Andrew Bolton thrust himself away from her and stood up.

In the half-dark of her sitting room, Nicky Piper clutched her elderly dressing gown round her. Andrew had arrived at midnight, bearing flowers and champagne. High on the success of a new contract and several hours celebrating it, he had woken her up, danced her sexily round her sitting room and then, laughing, carried her to the sofa.

Where they'd both come face to face with a truth they had been avoiding for months.

'Face it, Nicky. You don't want me.' The honesty was brutal. 'In your heart of hearts, you never have.'

Nicky ran her fingers through her loosened hair. In the light reflected from the street lamp outside her window stray fronds gleamed like diamonds. Even with all the gold leached out of it, the soft, curly mass was spectacular. Andrew eyed it broodingly.

'Oh, boy, did I want you,' he said, almost to himself. 'Gorgeous blonde. Legs to your eyebrows. Figure like a paradise houri.'

Nicky said nothing but her jaw ached with tension. Although she said nothing Andrew picked up on it at once. The look he sent her was wry.

'I know. I know. I'm not supposed to mention it.' His sigh sounded as if it was wrenched out of him. 'You're a lovely girl, Nicky. Why don't you want anyone to notice? Even when they're making love to you?'

Nicky shaded her eyes. This was truth indeed.

'I—tried.'

Andrew swung round on her. 'That's the point,' he said, suddenly fierce. 'You're not supposed to have to *try*.'

Nicky knew he was right. She hugged her knees to her chest, feeling guilty. She had so wanted to be in love with him. Until tonight she would have said she was. But all he had to do was to come to her when she was not expecting him and the façade cracked to pieces.

And suddenly there was the real Nicky—tense as a drum and armed to the teeth against invasion. And that was Andrew's problem—for all their shared laughter, when he took her by surprise, Nicky turned and saw an invader.

She said, half to herself, 'I didn't realise.'

He sat down on the bamboo chair under the window and looked at her. In the sodium light from the street lamp his expression was sombre.

'Someone has given you a real pasting, hasn't he?'

'No,' said Nicky, horrified.

It couldn't still hurt. It *couldn't*. Not after all these years. She had been a child then. Now she was a woman, independent and in control of her life. She couldn't still be in the power of something so *stupid*.

She knelt down in front of his chair and looked up into his face. 'Andrew, I'm so sorry.'

He touched her cheek, quite without his usual passion, his eyes searching her shadowed face.

'Have you ever been in love, Nicky?'

Nicky shrugged evasively. 'I don't know what you mean by love.'

'I mean,' said Andrew drily, 'has there ever been a man you wanted to make love with? Without pretending.'

And, fast as a lightning strike, Nicky thought, *He knows about Steve*. Her whole body juddered with the shock of it. And in that moment she gave herself away.

'I see,' said Andrew at length.

Nicky pulled herself together. She stood up.

'One adolescent crush,' she said drily. She was glad to

hear she sounded more like herself at last. 'Very adolescent and very short-lived.'

Andrew watched her. 'Returned?'

Nicky gave an unamused laugh. 'He despised me,' she said flatly. 'Very understandable. Looking back, I despise myself.' Her voice rasped.

Andrew was taken aback. 'Isn't that a bit extreme? For a teenage mistake?'

Nicky had told herself the same thing a million times. It made no difference. Every time she thought about Steve and what she had so nearly done with him, she wanted to hide.

'I made a fool of myself,' she said between her teeth. 'It's got nothing to do with you and me.'

'Hasn't it?'

He got up and touched her shoulder. Nicky's shoulders went rigid. His hand fell.

'You see?' said Andrew tiredly. 'It's got everything to do with you and me. And any other man who tries to get near you.'

'Don't say that,' protested Nicky involuntarily.

He said in a low voice, 'Nicky, I love you to bits but this is getting us nowhere.'

'But—'

'No!' he said forcefully. 'I don't want a girlfriend who braces herself every time I touch her.'

'I don't!'

He turned her round to face him. For a long moment, he looked searchingly into her eyes. Even in the half-dark his expression said as clearly as words that he could still hear what she could. High on his triumph, Andrew had been too excited to give her *time*, thought Nicky. And in that fatal instant when he had carried her to the sofa all the ancient horrors had crowded in. She did not know which of them had been more shocked by her animal cry of rejection.

Now, as she remembered, Nicky's hands flew to her burning cheeks.

Andrew said quietly, 'I deserve better than that, Nicky.'

There was a long, agonised pause. Nicky's hands fell.

'I know,' she said almost inaudibly.

'And, frankly, so do you.'

He looked round for his jacket. It was where he had thrown it, on the floor. The bottle of champagne he had brought lay on its side, half crushing the bright chrysanthemums he had found at the late-night store. Nicky blinked back sudden tears.

'I'm sorry.'

Andrew had behaved well but he was still smarting. 'So am I.'

He went to the door, then turned and kissed her cheek, quickly, with a new and awkward formality. Nicky leaned against him, burying her face in his chest so she did not have to see the pain in his eyes. He touched her hair fleetingly.

'If you want my advice, you'll find the guy. Get him out of your system. Or you'll never be free.'

He went.

Nicky put the chain on the door and leaned her back against it. She was too shaken for tears.

She had thought she loved Andrew. Well—she was too shaken for dishonesty as well—she had thought that Andrew would take her as close to love as she was ever likely to get. She had thought it would be enough. It had never occurred to her that she was cheating Andrew.

'Now what?' said Nicky aloud.

She had no idea of the answer.

CHAPTER ONE

IN THE morning, of course, things looked different. They always did, thought Nicky. There was a job to do, her brother to meet for lunch, the last sunshine of autumn to savour. The small things, as always, would carry her through.

'I will survive,' Nicky told her mirror.

The gorgeous reflection stared back, only partially convinced.

Why on earth do I look like this? she thought. Andrew was right when he said she was a fraud. Even in her sober business suit she looked the original party blonde. What was more, she always had. Nicky winced at the thought.

Of course, there had been changes over the years. When she was sixteen her skin had been golden with a Caribbean tan; her untamed hair used to be a sun-streaked lion's mane. These days she was city-pale and her daffodil hair shone. But, in spite of her best efforts, it was never quite immaculate. Soft tendrils always escaped to lie enticingly against her long neck. Add to that a kissable mouth and wide, long-lashed blue-grey eyes and it was not surprising that men looked at her and thought they had found their dream babe. Nicky bared her teeth at her reflection.

'Some babe,' she said bitterly.

She was still brooding when she got to work.

'Hey, what did I do?' said Martin de Vries in mock alarm.

Nicky jumped, conscience stricken. Martin was the boss of Springdown Kitchens and she was late for work. Now she'd compounded her sins by glaring at him. She shook her head ruefully.

'Nothing. It's just one of those Monday mornings, that's all.'

9

Martin nodded briskly. 'That's a relief. I need to get off to the exhibition hall soon.' But he hesitated. 'Are you sure you're all right?'

Damn, thought Nicky. Martin was an old friend of the family. Of course he could see right through the last twenty years to the six-year-old with scabby knees and pigtails. It gave him an unfair advantage.

She summoned up a bright smile. 'I'm fine.'

Martin knew how to interpret that. He had daughters of his own. He nodded. 'Boyfriend trouble,' he diagnosed.

Nicky winced theatrically. 'You sound like my mother.'

'No, I don't. I sound like a caring employer.'

'My next job is going to be with a hard-hearted tycoon who doesn't know a thing about his employees. And cares less,' Nicky muttered.

Martin ignored that. 'What's happened, Nick? Did he do something unforgivable, like want to marry you?'

Nicky smacked her conscience back in its box and glared at him for real.

'That's my business. Get down to the Lifestyle Fair and sell some kitchens,' she retorted.

Martin was torn. He was fond of Nicky. On the other hand he ran a vulnerable small business and the fair was the show-case of the year.

'As long as it isn't a crisis,' he said, patently anxious to be reassured.

Nicky gave a small huff of fury. But then genuine affection took over.

'No crisis,' she said more gently. 'Just something that's been building up a long time. All under control.'

'OK,' said Martin, relieved. He went.

Squaring up to the work on her desk, Nicky found that he had left her plenty to do. It was a relief. It took her mind off the uncomfortable truths Andrew had exposed last night.

Besides, she knew that what she was doing was worth-while. Martin was an inspired salesman, whereas Nicky liked practical organisation. She had her head down over the specifications of a small hotel kitchen when a cup appeared in front of her.

'Coffee,' said Caroline Leith, Martin's newest and most sophisticated assistant. 'You're going to need it.'

Nicky looked up. 'What's happened?'

'Martin refused to take any phone calls before he left.'

Nicky's heart sank. That meant clients who would already be annoyed when she called them back.

'Who?'

Caroline consulted her notebook. 'Two from Mr Tremain's secretary. One from Weber Hotels. Three from Mrs Van Linden. All of them only wanted to talk to Martin.' She grinned. 'Mrs Van Linden positively refused to talk to you under any circumstances. What happened? You told her what you thought of her horrible kitchen? Or she's seen how you look?'

Nicky raised her eyes to heaven. 'What's wrong with how I look?' she said dangerously.

'Nothing as long as you aren't a trophy wife worried about the competition.'

Nicky frowned. Caroline chuckled, unabashed.

'What do you expect, with a figure like yours?' she said frankly. 'It may be unfashionable to have all those curves but it sure as hell presses all the right male buttons.'

Nicky tensed. That was more or less exactly what Andrew had said last night. To say nothing of a man called Steve under a Caribbean moon... But the phone rang and broke that particular unwelcome train of thought.

Caroline answered it, listened, then put her hand over the receiver. 'SOS. Sally's in trouble. Sounds like she's going to cry.'

Nicky frowned blackly. Sally was the ideal receptionist, unfailingly sunny even with the most difficult clients. Anyone who reduced her to tears needed to be put in their place without delay. She held out an imperative hand.

'It's Tremain,' Caroline warned.

It gave Nicky pause for a moment. 'Who?'

'Tremain. Martin knows him personally. From the yacht club.'

Nicky scanned her memory. Nothing. She said so. 'But he's not going to bully Sally.'

'Kid-gloves time,' advised Caroline, surrendering the phone.

Nicky knew the warning tone was justified. She squared her shoulders and tried to remember the bit in her management course about dealing with difficult clients.

'I'm sorry to keep you waiting—' she began, uncharacteristically soothing.

'Then don't.' It was impatient and very male. At once she knew why Sally had not been able to calm him down. Mr Tremain did not want to be calmed down. Mr Tremain wanted blood.

And, true to form, it made Nicky want to fight right back. She curbed her combative instinct but it was a close-run thing.

'How can I—'

He did not let her finish. 'Where's de Vries?'

'—help you?' Sweet reason was not paying off. Well, then, she would give him a taste of her real reaction to a man who interrupted her twice. 'What can I do for you?' she finished, the frost showing.

Caroline did not go. Instead she propped herself up against a drawer of files and waited, prepared to be amused.

Mr Tremain was not impressed by Nicky's chilly formality. 'You can get me de Vries,' he said grimly. 'Now.'

'I'm afraid that's not poss—'

'Now.'

Nicky could feel her fuse shortening. Caroline grinned. Nicky frowned her down and raised her voice. 'If you would just let me finish—'

'I haven't got time to waste talking to lieutenants.' Even allowing for the distortion of the telephone, the dismissive tone was an insult. Nicky's fuse suddenly became very short indeed. And her frost dissolved into simple temper.

'Then try listening,' she flashed. 'Martin de Vries is not here. I can ask him to call you when he gets back or you can talk to me now. Your choice. Frankly I don't care which— but make up your mind. I haven't got time to waste either.'

Across the office, Caroline raised her eyebrows. Oh, *hell*, thought Nicky, remembering the management course too late.

But at least her outburst seemed to give Tremain pause.

He said slowly, 'Work closely with de Vries, do you?'

Nicky was all dignity. 'Of course.'

'So you're fully briefed on everything that's gone wrong with the blasted kitchen he sold me?'

'Well, I would have to look at the file...'

'And of *course* you're empowered to agree on compensation?' he went on sweetly.

Nicky knew quite well what he was doing. Silently she ground her teeth.

'I would have to consult Mr de Vries,' she conceded stiffly.

'Quite.' His tone was suddenly a lot less sweet. 'So let's stop playing games. We both know de Vries is ducking and weaving. Cut the feeble excuses, dig him out of wherever he's hiding and put him on the line *now*.'

If Nicky did not like being dismissed, she positively hated being patronised.

She yelled, 'I do not play games. I do not tell lies. And Martin isn't here.'

And banged the phone down.

Caroline gave her a slow, mocking hand-clap. 'That showed him.'

Nicky was steaming. 'So it should. Bully,' she threw at the phone, as if the man were there in person.

'Esteban Tremain must be shivering in his shoes,' murmured Caroline.

'Quite right too,' Nicky announced, militant. 'He shouldn't have tried to bully Sally. And he shouldn't have talked to me like that. I haven't got the time to take a lot of rubbish from people who don't listen. It's too close to lunchtime.'

She glanced at her watch as she spoke. She had a date with her brother and Ben had been known to leave a restaurant if people kept him waiting.

'Tell that to Martin when you explain how you handled his biggest problem client,' Caroline said with feeling.

Nicky stared. 'Biggest problem client? What are you talking about?'

'You mean you don't *know* who Esteban Tremain is?'

'Never met the man in my life,' said Nicky, adding darkly, 'And, on present showing, I'll be quite happy if that's the way it stays.'

'Stately home?' prompted Caroline. 'Cornwall? Try, gorgeous.'

'Oh, please!'

'You can't have forgotten him. A Savile Row suit with muscles. When he came in to the showroom every woman in the place wandered by for a look.'

Nicky shook her head. 'None of us is that sex-starved,' she protested, trying not to laugh. 'What is he? A film star?'

Caroline said in a practical tone, 'No. Just tall, dark and smouldering with sex appeal. And threatening to sue Martin for every penny he's got.'

'*What?*'

She cocked a mocking eyebrow. 'Come on, Nicky. The kitchen at Hallam Hall must have cost us more grief than any other contract this year.'

'Hallam Hall!' gasped Nicky, enlightened at last.

Now she knew exactly who Esteban Tremain was. And how much he could cost Springdown Kitchens if he put his mind to it.

'Oh, my Lord,' she said. 'Get the file into my office *now*.'

Caroline ran.

Esteban Tremain looked at the suddenly buzzing telephone with disbelief. Nobody cut him off. *Nobody.* He began to punch buttons savagely.

The door opened. 'Er—' said his secretary.

One glance was enough to tell her that he was in a temper. She did not think much of Francesca Moran's chances of getting in to see him when he looked like that.

Esteban glared at her across the telephone.

'What?'

'Miss Moran,' said Anne fast. Her tone was strictly neutral. 'She's been shopping. She wondered if you would like to take her to lunch.'

Esteban breathed hard.

Anne held her breath. When she'd come to work for him three years ago there had been plenty of people to warn her that Esteban would be impossible. He was a heart-breaker; he was a workaholic; he had a fiendish temper. She had learned that it was all true. Only he did not take any of it out on his secretary. Normally...

With an angry exclamation, he threw the telephone from him and flung out of his chair. Anne quietly restored the telephone to its cradle and waited.

Esteban strode up to the floor-length window. He thrust his hands into his pockets and glared out at the rain-lashed lawns. A muscle worked in his cheek.

Esteban wrestled with his temper. None of this was Anne's fault, he reminded himself. He gave an explosive sigh and swung back to the room.

'My regrets to Francesca,' he said rapidly, not sounding regretful at all. 'Anything else?'

Anne, the perfect secretary, did not protest. She just said carefully, 'I'll go along and tell her you're too busy to see her, shall I?'

There was a small, sizzling pause.

'She's here?'

'I'm afraid so.'

'But I told her last time—' He remembered again that it was not Anne's fault and stopped. *'Damn.'*

Esteban thought, then took one of his famous lightning decisions. 'OK. You'd better wheel her in for a bit. But not long.'

He reached for his jacket.

Esteban never received visitors in his shirt sleeves, Anne thought. Not even a lady he regularly spent the night with. Though she was not sure that Francesca Moran was in that category these days, in spite of the gossip or, indeed, the hints that Miss Moran herself let fall so heavily.

'I'll just clear a space,' murmured Anne, again the perfect secretary, advancing on a tower of papers.

Esteban looked around his room in faint surprise. Apart from the papers that covered his desk, there were two large books open on the floor beside him and piles of more papers that needed his attention on every one of his comfortable chairs. He looked amused suddenly.

'Don't bother.'

'But she's got to have somewhere to sit.'

'Why? It will only encourage her,' said Esteban wickedly.

He flicked his lapels straight. Looking up, he gave her a conspiratorial grin.

'Buzz me in five, max. Right?'

'Right,' said Anne.

Francesca Moran, she thought with satisfaction, would be back in the rainy garden a lot sooner than she expected. Anne did not like Francesca.

It would have been impossible to tell from Esteban's manner whether he liked her or not. He kissed her on both exquisitely made up cheeks in welcome. But he adroitly avoided her move to deepen the embrace and retired behind the bulwark of his desk. Francesca accepted the rebuff as gracefully as if she had not recognised it. She took up a perch on the arm of an ancient leather chair and gave him a sweet smile.

'We need to talk,' she said caressingly.

Esteban raised his eyebrows. 'Oh?'

Francesca's myopic grey eyes made her look vague and fragile. It was misleading.

'Yes. I was thinking all the time I was in Cornwall. It's

stupid for us to be like this. We ought to let bygones be bygones and pool our resources.'

Esteban's poker face was famous. But for a moment he could not contain his astonishment. At once, he controlled his expression. But one corner of his mouth twitched.

'Are you proposing to me, Francesca?' he asked politely.

She was not disconcerted. She batted her eyelashes and gave him a smile of calculated charm.

'Well, you're not going to propose to me, are you?'

Esteban was surprised into laughing aloud. 'You're right there,' he agreed, watching her with fascination.

Francesca shrugged. 'So it's up to me,' she said with no sign of rancour. 'You need a wife. It would be ideal.'

'I'm afraid I don't, you know,' said Esteban. He was gentle but quite firm.

But Francesca, as he had learned in Gibraltar last year, did not recognise firmness when it meant someone not doing what she wanted.

'It would be perfect,' she said, unheeding. 'The time is right for both of us.'

Esteban leaned back in his chair and surveyed her in disbelief. She smiled back, not discouraged. He decided to try another tack.

'What makes you think I need a wife?' he drawled.

She gestured round the untidy room. 'You're in a complete mess. You need someone to run the practical side of your life so that you can get on with your career.'

'That's what Anne does,' he objected.

'Don't be ridiculous, darling. That's not what I meant and you know it.'

'Then explain,' he said blandly.

Francesca refused to be annoyed. 'You're being silly,' she said in an indulgent tone. 'What about your private life? Where would you have been if I hadn't gone down to Hallam Hall and sorted out those workmen?'

'Ah. I wondered when that would come up,' said Esteban with satisfaction.

Francesca frowned. 'You would have been lost without me,' she said, her tone sharpening. 'You were out of the country and those cowboys were getting away with murder.'

'And I was grateful for your help but—'

Francesca regained her good humour. 'I bet you haven't even talked to the kitchen people yet.'

Esteban looked at the telephone. His expression darkened. He was not going to admit to Francesca that the woman had hung up on him. Why did women always have to play *games*?

'I've got it in hand,' he said brusquely.

Francesca got up and came over to him. A faint hint of expensive scent wafted as she settled herself on the corner of the desk beside him. She crossed one leg over the other and smiled down into his eyes.

'Don't you see, darling? Marry me and you would never have to deal with kitchen designers again.'

Her high-heeled shoe tapped at his thigh to emphasise her point.

'An alluring prospect,' said Esteban drily.

He pushed his chair back, removing his immaculate suit out of range.

'And you need a hostess,' Francesca went on, her smile unwavering. 'Someone to organise the dinner parties, make sure you meet the right people.'

He almost shuddered.

'I don't think so.'

'Of course you do.'

She would have gone on but Esteban put an end to it. He stood up and looked down at her, all vestige of amusement gone.

'I thought I had been clear, Francesca. If you misunderstood me, I'm sorry. But the truth is that my stepfather needs a housekeeper. You said you wanted a job. A job is all that's on offer.'

'But—'

'If you remember,' Esteban said drily, 'I said at the time

I thought you would find Hallam very isolated. But you wanted to give it a shot.'

Francesca's mouth thinned. For a moment the pretty face looked almost ugly.

'Are you saying you used me?'

Esteban stiffened imperceptibly. 'Excuse me?'

There were people—witnesses for the prosecution, say, or opposing counsel—who would have run a mile when he spoke in that soft tone. Francesca did not read the danger signals. She tossed her head.

'Of course I adore Patrick,' she said unconvincingly. 'I was very willing to *help*—'

Esteban said quietly, 'You wanted a job.'

Francesca did not like that. 'You know quite well what I wanted,' she said sharply.

It was a moment of total self-betrayal. There was a nasty silence. Francesca bit her lip.

Esteban said heavily, 'I seem to have been very stupid. I thought you knew that all that was over. I told you so last year.'

'Darling, just because of a silly article in a magazine—'

He stopped her with an upraised hand. 'It was not about the article. I don't care what some tinpot journalist writes about me.'

'Well, then—'

'But I care that someone I trusted talked to a tinpot journalist,' Esteban went on softly. 'About stuff I told you in confidence.'

There was another nasty silence. Francesca watched him, frustrated.

At last she burst out, 'It's such a stupid *waste*. I could really help your career. Daddy's contacts—a bit of networking—'

'And what about love?' he said wryly.

'Love?' Francesca sounded as blank as if he had broken into a foreign language. 'Grow up, darling.'

'You think love's an irrelevance?'

'Oh, come on. We're talking real life here.'

Esteban gave an unexpected laugh. 'We are indeed. And we seem to have different views on it.'

'Are you saying you're looking for love?' Francesca sounded disbelieving. 'You?'

'I don't think you need to look for it,' Esteban said coolly. 'In my experience it tends to sock you in the eye.'

Francesca snorted. 'Your experience? So now you're the last of the great romantics?'

Esteban gave that his measured consideration. 'No,' he said at last. 'I wouldn't call myself a romantic.'

'Thank God for that, at least,' Francesca muttered.

'On the other hand, I'm not fool enough to marry anyone I'm not in love with.'

Francesca pulled herself together. She moved close to him, though she did not quite dare to touch him again. She gave him a winning smile.

'But if both parties agree—'

He bent towards her so fast she took a step backwards in simple shock. At once she could have kicked herself. He had not come so close to her voluntarily for over a year.

But it was too late. Esteban had seen her alarm. He gave her a mocking smile.

'Agree to change my nature? How?'

Francesca recovered fast. 'But you've just said you aren't romantic,' she reminded him.

'No, but I am passionate and possessive and I have a nasty temper,' Esteban told her evenly. 'Believe me, you wouldn't like being married to me.'

'No woman would,' snapped Francesca, unexpectedly shaken.

He raised his eyebrows. 'I'm glad we agree on the matter.' He sounded amused.

The telephone rang. He reached behind him, not looking, and swept it up to his ear. 'Hi, Annie. Now? Yes, of course.' He put the phone down. 'Sorry, Francesca. Busy morning. Goodbye.'

Francesca was looking poleaxed. His court opponents would have recognised the feeling. Esteban gave her an enigmatic smile and held the door open for her. She did not move.

'You're not going to treat me like this. I'm no little boat chick,' she jeered.

Esteban went very still. Francesca knew she had made a bad mistake. That was one of the few confidences she had not spilled out to the handsome young journalist in the quayside café last year.

She nervously touched her hair but said defiantly, 'It just slipped out. You told me about it yourself, after all. I couldn't help it. You upset me so much I forgot I wasn't supposed to mention it.' A thought occurred to her. She lowered her lashes. 'If you go on being nasty to me, it might happen again—and who knows who could be listening?'

Esteban's watchfulness dissolved into unholy appreciation.

'Threats?' he said, his eyebrows flying up. 'Very attractive. Just the stuff to get me to marry you. You're really one on your own, Francesca.'

There was nothing she could say. Once again Esteban Tremain had taken her well thought out strategy and turned it on its head. Francesca was determined but she was not an idiot. She recognised defeat, at least for the moment.

'I'll go.' She gathered up her handbag and elegant serape but was not leaving without the last word. 'Call me when you've got your head together. You need me.'

'I don't think so,' Esteban said quietly.

'Oh, but you do.' She had gone back to her caressing manner. She gave him a sweet smile. 'You just don't know how much yet. But you will.'

She left.

Immediately Esteban banished her from his mind. He flung himself back into his chair and reached for the Hallam file again. He picked up the telephone, his voice coming alive with the anticipation of battle.

'Annie, get me that kitchen place again, will you? And this time I want to talk to de Vries in person.'

But when Anne put the call through it was the lieutenant again.

'Hello?' She did her best to sound composed but Esteban was used to reading the smallest nuance in his opponents' voices and he recognised nerves. It was a lovely voice, Esteban noted, warm with an underlying hint of laughter. Currently, of course, the laughter was almost extinguished. *Good*, he thought.

'What is your name?' he demanded softly.

He did not have to say anything else. The tone alone intimidated opponents. Esteban knew it and used it effectively in court. If it could silence Francesca Moran, a judge's daughter, it would make this obstructive girl crumble.

But, to his astonishment, it did not. There was a little pause, in which he could almost hear her pull herself together.

Then, 'Piper,' she said coolly. 'Nicola Piper.' She spelled it for him.

It disconcerted him. Esteban was not used to hostile witnesses spelling out their names and then asking kindly if he had got it all down. Where had she got that kind of confidence? Did he know her? Surely he would not have forgotten that golden sunshine voice?

'Have we met?' he asked slowly.

Nicky had remembered his visit as soon as Caroline had mentioned Hallam Hall. She had just come in from dealing with another client. And she had noticed him all right: a tall, dark man in the doorway of Martin's office, watching her with lazy appreciation.

'You could say that. In passing,' she said frostily.

That startled him too. And intrigued him. 'Where did we pass?'

'At the office. We weren't introduced.'

There was a thoughtful pause.

'You're the blonde,' Esteban said on a long note of discovery.

He remembered now. She had shot in from somewhere, silk skirts flying, laughing. Her briefcase had bulged with papers and she'd been clutching it under one arm with decreasing effectiveness. He would have gone to rescue it, but Martin had detained him with some remark and one of her colleagues had got there first.

This picture was still vivid, though. Summer evening sun had lit her hair to gold. It had clearly started the day confined in a neat bow at her nape but by now it was springing free into wild curls about her shoulders. And her figure— Esteban found his mouth curving in appreciation at the memory. She had a figure to rival one of Patrick's Renaissance goddesses at Hallam, lounging in naked voluptuousness among their sunlit olive groves. Add to that perfect legs, creamy skin— and, when she'd caught his eyes on her—a glare like a stiletto.

'I remember,' he said.

Alone in her office, Nicky winced. It was not the first time a man had called her a 'blonde' in that tone of voice. Or looked at her in blatant appreciation, as she now remembered all too clearly. It still stabbed where she was most vulnerable. Particularly this morning.

She hid her hurt under icy distance. 'The *name*,' she said with emphasis, 'is Piper.'

'Is it, indeed?'

Nicky could hear his amusement. She set her teeth and tried to remember that he was a customer.

He went on, 'Well, Piper, you can tell Martin de Vries that I paid for a working kitchen and that's what I expect to get.'

Nicky was bewildered. In spite of what Caroline had said, the file had been clear. Admittedly, there had been complaint after complaint but they all seemed to have been dealt with. Moreover, the complainant was not Mr Tremain. The name on the telephoned demands was a Ms Francesca Moran.

In response, machinery had been tested and tested again, cabinets resited, floor tiling replaced. A month ago, Tremain had threatened legal action. But as far as Nicky could see all the disputed work on the Cornish mansion had been completed ten days before.

'Do you have another complaint?' she said warily.

'Complaint!' His derisive bark of laughter made her eardrums ring.

Nicky held the phone away from her head until he had finished.

'Would you like to be more specific?' she suggested sweetly, when she thought he might be able to hear her again.

'Gladly.' He launched into a list.

Nicky listened in gathering disbelief.

'Don't be ridiculous,' she said when he finished. 'That would mean every single appliance had gone wrong.'

'Precisely,' said Esteban Tremain.

In her astonishment Nicky forgot she had decided she loathed the man.

'But they can't have done. They've been checked. And they're *new*.'

'I certainly paid for new machines,' he agreed suavely.

Nicky took a moment to assimilate that. 'Are you suggesting—?'

He interrupted again. 'My dear girl, I am suggesting nothing.'

Of course, he was a lawyer, Nicky remembered with dislike. He knew exactly how to hint without actually accusing her or Springdown Kitchens of anything precise enough to be actionable.

Her voice shaking with fury, she said, 'I object to the implication.'

'Implication?' His voice was smooth as cream. 'What implication was that?'

'Springdown Kitchens honour their contracts,' Nicky said hotly. 'If we charge you for new appliances, you get new appliances. You're accusing us of installing substandard machines—'

'Stop right there.' It sliced across her tumbling speech like an ice axe. 'I'm not accusing anyone of anything. Yet.'

Just that single word brought Nicky to a halt. She looked at her hand, gripping the telephone convulsively, and saw that she was shaking. Justified indignation, she assured herself.

But it did not feel like justified indignation. It felt as if she was a schoolgirl in a tantrum, not a serious professional dealing with an awkward client. Nicky breathed deeply.

She said, 'You'd better take this up with Mr de Vries.'

'As you may recall,' Esteban Tremain said blandly, 'that was exactly what I wanted to do in the first place.'

Nicky could not take any more. 'I'll tell him to call you as soon as I can catch him,' she said curtly.

And flung the phone down before she screamed.

This time he did not call back.

It had made her late, of course. She had promised Ben she would be there at twelve-fifteen at the latest, before the little bistro filled up with the lunchtime trade. Ben hated to be crowded. Just as he hated to wait. Impatience ran in the family.

Nicky gathered up her coat and bag with clumsy fingers. Caroline, having seen the phone call and its effect, wandered in.

'Tremain again, I take it. That man thinks he only has to crook his little finger.' She raised an eyebrow. 'What are you going to do?'

'Have lunch,' said Nicky, scribbling furiously on Martin's notepad, just in case he came back during the lunch break.

Caroline was intrigued. 'A date?'

Nicky tore off the note she had penned and stuck it over the top of Martin's phone where he could not miss it, no matter how hard he tried. She looked up.

'What price respect for personal privacy?' she asked resignedly.

'Never heard of it,' Caroline said with a grin. Nicky bared her teeth and dived past her.

'What will I do if Martin calls?' Caroline yelled after her.

'Tell him everything,' Nicky called back. 'It's all in the note. Tell him I'll deal with it if he wants. But not before lunch.'

She flung herself at the showroom door. Caroline followed her, grinning.

'And what if the frustrated client turns up in person?'

A wicked light invaded Nicky's eyes.

'Tell Mr Tremain he'll have to wait. I'm lunching with a man who won't.'

CHAPTER TWO

HER brother was waiting outside the bistro, lost in thought. Nicky broke into a run, calling his name. Ben looked up. He surged towards her, cleaving his way through the lunchtime crowd, and flung his arms wide.

It was an old joke. But Nicky felt oddly weepy as she ran full-tilt into them. Ben swung her off her feet with a rebel yell. Even on a rainy autumn street, dense with lunchtime crowds, heads turned; people smiled. He was so handsome, so full of life. He threw her into the air, looking up at her with a devilish grin.

'Put me down,' gasped Nicky. She was breathless, between laughter and unaccountable tears.

Ben only noticed the laughter. He returned her to the pavement and held her at arm's length, surveying her appreciatively.

'You look great,' he said. 'Even if you're late.'

'I know. I know,' she said placatingly. 'Sorry, I hit a natural disaster. Let's eat.'

The waiter showed them to the small corner table for which Nicky had managed to wrest a reservation out of the management. He brought them water and menus and a carafe of wine while Nicky regaled Ben with the account of her battles with the difficult client.

It entertained him hugely.

'Don't know about a natural disaster. It sounds to me as if you've met your match,' he said when she finished.

Nicky bridled. 'Oh, no, I haven't. He just—took me by surprise, that's all.'

'It's the only way,' murmured Ben teasingly.

Nicky sent him a look that would have crushed him if he had been anyone but her brother. He laughed.

'It's good for you,' he said hardily. 'You've been getting downright bossy.'

Nicky laughed. They both knew what he meant.

Ben was twenty-eight to her twenty-six but sometimes she felt as if he was still a teenager. He had been in London for three years, living a rollercoaster life. One day he was living in the lap of luxury with an old mate and earning a fortune. The next, he was standing on Nicky's doorstep at three in the morning without even the wherewithal to pay the taxi that had brought him.

Nicky always paid the cab, gave him a bed for the night and a loan to tide him over. It never took long. Normally Ben was on his way up again within a week.

He repaid her scrupulously and, as often as not, took her somewhere wildly expensive to celebrate the revival of his fortunes. And then she would not see him again until there was something else to celebrate or he was back at the bottom of the ride again. In fact Nicky had been wondering ever since he rang which it was this time.

But she knew him too well to ask a direct question. Instead, she let him pour wine for them both.

'You know, sometimes I feel like a changeling,' she said suddenly.

'You?' Ben paused, the carafe poised over his glass. He looked across at her in unfeigned surprise. 'But you're the only sensible one in the family.'

'Quite.'

'You mean the parents are rogues and vagabonds and I'm a financial disaster,' he interpreted.

Nicky shook her head.

'No. I mean you're relaxed. Free. You don't have to plan everything.'

Ben shrugged. 'So you're a planner. Somebody has to be.' He chuckled suddenly. 'The parents didn't do so well without you running the itinerary, did they?'

Nicky was startled into a little crow of laughter. When she'd moved to England eight years ago, her parents had announced that now, at last, they were going to sail round the world. But between one thing and another they had not quite set out yet.

Ben leaned across and patted her hand.

'So don't knock yourself just because you have some common sense.' His expression darkened. 'I wish to God I'd been as sensible.'

Nicky was concerned. 'Problems? Can I—?'

But he shook his head decisively. 'No. I can't keep touching you every time I'm short. Anyway, I've got something to keep me going while I sort myself out.'

Nicky did not argue. She knew his pride. So she just said, 'What do you think you'll do?'

He pulled a face. 'Winter's coming. I'm tempted to go south, see if I can get some sailing. There's bound to be a gin palace looking for a crew somewhere.'

Nicky could not repress her sudden shudder. Ben raised an eyebrow enquiringly.

'You mean a boat like the *Calico Jane*?'

Ben grinned. 'Hardly. Showiest boat in the Caribbean. Too many electronics for me. What made you think of her?'

She shrugged, regretting her unwary question.

But the name had awakened a forgotten mystery and Ben was not going to let it go.

'Was she the one, then? When you went moonlighting?' He laughed reminiscently. 'God, Mum was furious.'

'It was a long time ago,' Nicky said repressively.

The summer she was sixteen. It could have been yesterday.

Ben was intrigued. 'What did happen? I never knew.'

Nicky shrugged again, not answering. She found that Ben was looking at her in sudden speculation.

'You know, back then you were a babe to die for.'

That was more or less what they had said on board *Calico Jane*. Nicky could feel the colour leave her face. Fortunately, Ben was too taken up with his sudden memories to notice.

'My friends were always on at me to bring you to parties.' He grinned, remembering. 'It used to drive me mad.' He looked at her, shaking his head sorrowfully. 'Who would have thought you'd turn into a wage slave? You were born to be a party girl.'

In spite of herself, Nicky choked. 'I have a living to earn,' she pointed out drily.

Ben put his head on one side and smiled the charming smile that had girlfriends falling over themselves to share his bed and do his laundry. 'You can earn a living and still have some fun, you know.'

'I do. It's just that your idea of fun and mine is different.'

Ben flung up his hands.

'I give in. You will live and die a businesswoman. And the wildest day of your week will be the girls' night out.'

Since Ben had met all her friends and, indeed, made a spirited attempt to lure at least one of them into his sex and laundry net, Nicky did not take this slight too seriously.

'I want wild, I'll call my brother,' she said tartly.

And that, for some reason, silenced Ben.

Their food came. Slowly they eased back into their normal easy gossip about family and friends and her despised job.

'What's Martin going to say when he finds you've savaged one of his customers this morning?' Ben teased.

Nicky pulled a face. 'Any savaging that took place was in the other direction. You should have heard the way that man called me a ''blonde''.'

Ben laughed aloud. 'But you are a blonde. And gorgeous with it.'

'Not in the way he meant it,' said Nicky, ungrateful for the compliment. 'He made it sound as if all blondes are empty-headed nymphomaniacs.'

Ben waved his fork at her. 'And too ready to go to war. All you needed to do was sweet-talk him a little. The man would be eating out of your hand by now.'

'What a horrible thought,' Nicky retorted. 'Esteban Tremain is not the sort of man you sweet-talk lightly.'

The effect on Ben was electric. He sat bolt upright, his eyes narrowing. 'What?'

Nicky was faintly surprised. She amplified, 'If I have to butter up some man, at least let it be someone I can like.'

Ben ignored that. '*Who* did you say?'

'Esteban Tremain,' said Nicky, puzzled. 'Do you know him?'

That commanding voice had nothing in common with her erratic brother. She could not imagine how they could have met.

'I've heard of him,' said Ben, suddenly grim.

'And you don't like what you've heard,' Nicky interpreted.

It did not surprise her. Ben was easygoing to a fault but he would not take kindly to Tremain's habit of ordering everyone around. He was like his sister in that, at least.

'I've never met the man,' he said curtly. 'But—' He broke off, looking disturbed.

Nicky was intrigued. Not much worried her casual brother.

'But—?' she prompted.

He still hesitated, clearly torn.

At last he said, 'He's an ugly customer, from what I've heard. Steer clear of him.' He sounded serious.

Nicky was touched. She reached across the table and covered the back of his hand reassuringly.

'Don't worry. He's Martin's client. Martin can deal with him.' But she could not resist adding naughtily, 'So cancel the advice on sweet-talking him, then?'

Ben's frown disappeared in a great shout of laughter.

'Sharp,' he said when he could speak. 'Very sharp.'

The beep of Nicky's mobile phone interrupted them. She pulled it out of her capacious bag and flicked the switch.

'Hello?'

It was Caroline. 'Told you,' she said smugly. 'He's *here*. He virtually went through the broom cupboard looking for Martin.'

Nicky sniffed. 'Well, at least now he knows I was telling

the truth about Martin being out of the office. Did you call him? When will he be back?'

'Not this evening,' said Caroline with gloomy satisfaction. 'Better get back here before Tremain starts throwing things.'

Nicky looked at Ben apologetically. He nodded.

'Duty calls, eh? Fine. I'll walk you back.'

He did. And then, to her surprise, he slid one arm possessively round her waist and strolled into the showroom beside her.

Caroline came towards them. 'He's in Martin's office.'

Nicky looked across the showroom. A tall figure was pacing behind Martin's glass walls. As she looked, he stopped, turned, went still... Their eyes locked.

Nicky felt her heart give an odd lurch. It was like catching sight of someone she recognised; someone very important. Hardly knowing what she did, she removed herself from Ben's encircling arm. She did not take her eyes off that still figure.

Behind her Ben said, 'So that's Esteban Tremain.' He sounded as if he was committing him to memory.

The man left Martin's office and came swiftly across to her. His eyes never left her face. Nicky thought, *He knows me too.* She felt as if the earth's crust was suddenly gaping, leaving Ben and Caroline on the far side of the gulf, and Nicky and Esteban Tremain alone.

She blinked. Ben muttered something. She hardly heard him. Esteban Tremain paid no attention to anyone but Nicky. She shuddered under the intensity of those dark eyes.

I am not afraid, Nicky told herself.

Esteban Tremain said, 'So we meet at last, Nicola Piper.'

It broke the spell. She shook her head and the world came back into its proper focus.

At her shoulder, Ben said warningly, 'Nick?'

Esteban transferred his dark gaze. His eyes narrowed. He sized Ben up in silence.

They were a total contrast. In his well-cut suit, dark brows knit in frowning concentration, Esteban Tremain gave an impression of overwhelming power, only just contained. Ben meanwhile lounged against a pillar like a Greek god, all streaked blond hair and tanned forearms. Esteban Tremain stiffened.

Sheer panic found Nicky's tongue for her. 'Mr Tremain,' she said breathlessly. She held out her hand to him with more friendliness than she would have believed possible an hour ago.

He ignored her hand.

'I wouldn't want to interrupt your social life,' he said with awful courtesy.

Nicky frowned. She turned back to her brother.

'See you soon, Ben,' she said meaningfully.

'What?'

Nicky resisted the urge to tread heavily on his foot.

'I will be in touch,' she said between her teeth. She backed him to the door and opened it pointedly. 'Goodbye.'

Ben went reluctantly, with a long look over his shoulder at Esteban Tremain. It was almost menacing and totally out of character.

But Nicky had no time to think about that. Squaring her shoulders, she turned to deal with the most difficult client of her career to date.

Esteban Tremain did not acknowledge Ben's departure. But his displeasure was dissolving, she saw. It was replaced by sheer interest. He looked her up and down.

'So I was right,' he said softly. And smiled. Not kindly.

Nicky watched the curve of the sensual mouth and felt a hollow open up in the pit of her stomach. She moistened suddenly dry lips. He was looking at her the way she imagined Victorian naturalists looked at a new species of penguin, she thought. Delighted, amused—and quite unconcerned about the feelings of the penguin.

How could a man make you want to run and hide from him just by looking at you?

Nicky cleared her throat. 'Right about what?'

'Blonde,' Esteban said.

And smiled right into her eyes.

It caught her on the raw. But Nicky was not going to let him see that. She gave what was meant to be a light laugh. Then wished she hadn't, as the dark gaze transferred, pleasurably, to her breasts.

Nicky resisted the desire to hold the lapels of her jacket tight up to her throat. She pulled herself together with an effort.

'I can't deny it,' she said lightly.

She realised that they were attracting an interested audience. Once again Esteban Tremain had proved an irresistible draw to every girl in the place. They had all found jobs which brought them into the main showroom and were now busily engaged in them, ears flapping. Sally was gaping unashamedly.

Hurriedly Nicky said, 'Why don't we go into Martin's office?'

Esteban Tremain took in the audience with one comprehensive glance. He looked amused.

'By all means, if it makes you feel safer.'

Nicky set her teeth and reminded herself that her management course had taught her how to deal with all sorts of difficult clients, even sexy and amused ones. She led the way, trying to ignore the fact that it felt as if every eye in the showroom was burning between her shoulder blades. She decided she loathed Esteban Tremain heartily.

He followed close on her heels. Too close. As she stood aside to let him precede her, she breathed in his cologne. A shocking wave of something like memory hit her. The sea, she thought. He smells of the sea.

She swallowed and shut the door of Martin's glass case of an office with a bang that made the walls tremble.

Esteban Tremain frowned. He looked intrigued and annoyed in equal measure. But there was a simmering attraction there as well.

Out of nowhere the thought came: He's going to touch me. And, for no reason, the memory of Andrew's words last night came back to her, disastrous in their clarity. 'You'll never be free.'

Nicky had a moment of pure unreasoning panic. He saw it. Startled awareness leaped into Esteban's eyes. He seemed on the point of stepping towards her and her breath stopped in her throat.

Then steep eyelids hid his expression. He shoved his hands hard in his pockets. And Nicky's famous common sense kicked in.

She said rapidly, 'I'm afraid I haven't had the chance to talk to Mr de Vries yet. You can't expect—'

He said abruptly, almost as if the subject now bored him, 'None of those damned machines work. Sort it.'

Nicky clenched her hands. In her previous dealings with dissatisfied clients she was used to complaints about builders who did not work fast enough or colour schemes that their originators were now regretting. This sort of complaint about the appliances was a new one. She had not understood it when she'd read the file and she did not understand it now. Until she talked to Martin she did not know what to do about it.

Frowning, she said, 'Did you read the instructions properly?'

Esteban Tremain looked at her for an incredulous moment. Nicky realised she had made a mistake. She added hurriedly, 'I mean *all* the appliances going wrong. The statistical chances of that must be off the graph. Surely you can see that.'

He gave her a sweet, poisonous smile.

'Oh, I do. I can only conclude that it is not chance.'

Nicky was so bewildered by that, she did not even take offence at his tone.

'No one else has had a problem. Martin uses only the very best suppliers,' she said, thinking aloud. 'And even if one supplier has suddenly lost the plot on quality control we didn't get everything in your kitchen from just one company.

There were too many machines.' She looked up. 'You're sure every one of them was bad?'

Esteban Tremain looked down his nose. It was a thin, aquiline nose and it made her think of a particularly dictatorial Roman Emperor.

'I have not test-driven every waste-disposal unit and coffee-grinder, if that's what you mean.'

Nicky began to feel a little better.

'Well, which have you test-driven?' she demanded. That did not come out quite as she intended either. It sounded downright truculent.

His eyebrows, she noted irrelevantly, were very dark and fine. Just at the moment they were locked together across the bridge of his nose in a mighty frown. A Roman Emperor in a mood to condemn a gladiator.

'I am informed,' he said with precision, 'that neither the dishwasher nor the fridge/freezer are in working order. As a result my companion did not have the opportunity to test the oven to its fullest. However, her observation and my own lead us both to the conclusion that the oven is not working either.'

Nicky was not going to admit it but she was impressed. She also noted that Esteban Tremain delegated investigations of the fridge and the dishwasher to a female companion. She suspected that he shared Ben's ideas about the relationship between women, laundry and sex. Though Mr Tremain would undoubtedly present it in a more sophisticated manner. She did her best not to glower at him.

'Well, that is of course very serious.' She riffled through Martin's desk drawer for a notepad. 'Let me make a note—'

Esteban Tremain strolled forward.

'No more notes.'

He sounded quite pleasant. But, looking up, Nicky realised that he was a lot closer than she wanted him to be. And that he was in a cold rage. It must have been that rage which made her heart lurch, then start pounding so hard she was sure he must hear it.

He said gently, 'I didn't take the time out to come here so you could take more notes. This kitchen has taken four months longer than de Vries estimated. Hasn't it?'

The question somehow demanded an answer. Nicky could not help but nod. She knew from her reading of the file that he was right.

She could feel sweat breaking out along her spine. It was not fear. It was not, God help her, attraction. But it had some of the symptoms of both. She breathed carefully, praying that he would not notice.

'So what do you want?' she asked.

Esteban Tremain smiled dangerously and Nicky hung on to her pleasant expression, but it was an effort.

'I want action,' he said softly.

There was a sharp silence which Nicky did not entirely understand.

Struggling for normality, she said in a placating tone, 'So do we all. But there has to be some planning—'

True to form, Esteban Tremain did not waste time listening to her.

'I don't just mean as a general principle, some time in the future,' he explained, still in that chillingly friendly tone. 'I mean here and now. Today.'

He sounded cool and amused and as if he did not care one way or the other. Which was odd, considering the trouble he had caused. And her own instinctive feeling that he was so angry he could barely contain himself.

It took real courage to say drily, 'I don't do magic.'

For a moment his eyes flickered. Then he gave her a charming smile. It really was chilling.

'Then I won't ask for magic,' he said softly. 'Just my kitchen working like it's supposed to. Now, I suggest you personally get into your car and go—and—put—it—right.'

She was not deceived by the gentle tone.

'I can't do that at a moment's notice,' she protested. Esteban Tremain looked her up and down. Slowly. It was a deliberate put-down and they both knew it. Nicky felt the shamed heat rise in her cheeks. She *hated* him.

Her chin came up and she glared back at him, right into those dark, dark eyes. It amused him. One eyebrow rose enquiringly.

'Do you mend machinery by remote control, then?' he asked pleasantly.

Horribly conscious of her blazing cheeks, Nicky said curtly, 'Don't be ridiculous.'

'Then I suggest you do as I ask. And sooner rather than later. My secretary will sort out the arrangements.'

He paused, waiting. But Nicky was speechless. With a faint triumphant smile, Esteban Tremain walked out of the office.

On a surge of fury she had never felt before, Nicky picked up the Waterford ornament and threw it. Hard. It did not break but it brought in the watchers hot foot.

'What did he *say*?' demanded Sally, half shocked, half thrilled.

'What are you going to do?' asked the more practical Caroline, returning the small glass sculpture to Martin's desk.

'Is it damaged?' asked Nicky. Restored to herself, she was a little conscience-stricken.

'It bounced,' Caroline reassured her cheerfully. 'Tremain really got you wound up, didn't he? Tea, that's what you need.'

And while Sally went to get it Caroline produced a photocopied sheet from behind her back.

'Read this,' she said with relish.

It was a copy of a gossip column piece, dated nearly a year earlier. Headed 'Heart Throb Wins Again', it described a yacht race in the Mediterranean. Nicky read it aloud.

'Brilliant bachelor barrister Esteban Tremain's winning streak continues. After recent notable victories in court, he and his crew on *Glen Tandy* have won the Sapphire Cup. Famously elusive, these days the Latin Lover, as the Law

Courts call him, is spending time with very good friend Francesca, the popular daughter of Lord Moran. Friends say that Esteban does not tolerate criticism but he will have to smarten up his client list if he is going to tie the knot with a judge's daughter.'

Nicky looked up. 'What does that mean?'

'It means he's made mincemeat of better adversaries than you. Let Martin deal with him.'

'Do you know him, then?' said Nicky suspiciously.

Caroline had been brought in by Martin when the business had begun to expand and she was older than the others by several years. As a result, she had become the office guru. She did not disappoint now.

'Friends in common,' she said airily. 'He is some sort of Latin American by birth but he was quite young when his mother remarried so he was brought up in England and took his stepfather's name. He's as tough as they come. Always has to be in control.'

Nicky thought of those unfathomable eyes, so dark, so guarded. She shivered.

'I can believe it.'

'Don't try and handle this one yourself,' Caroline advised shrewdly. 'It's Martin's baby. Make him come back and deal with it.'

Nicky tried. It got her nowhere. Oh, Martin came back from the exhibition hall, all right. But by the time Nicky got in to see him he had already returned Esteban's calls and his expression was sober.

'Do what the man wants, Nick,' Martin said, before she had managed more than a couple of sentences.

Nicky stared.

'Have you listened to a word I've said?' she demanded.

'All of them.' Martin had had a hard day and it showed. He pushed a weary hand through untidy grey hair. 'You don't like Tremain and you think I should run him off the territory. Well, tough. For one thing, I haven't got the time. For another—we agreed when I took you on that that was your job. You do the trouble-shooting.'

'Not this sort of trouble-shooting.'

'Any sort of trouble-shooting,' Martin said firmly.

'You said yourself, I'm no good with clients,' Nicky pointed out.

This was true. On at least one occasion, Nicky had been so forthright that the client in question had banged out of the showroom, slamming the door so hard behind her that its handsome glass insets had cracked. Martin had laughed. But he had also said, 'It's safer to keep you away from the paying customers, isn't it?' Watching him woo back the offended client afterwards, Nicky could only agree.

Now she decided to remind him. 'Remember Mrs Lazenby?'

Martin remained infuriatingly unmoved.

'Jennifer Lazenby is a woman with too much time on her hands and not enough brain cells to know what to do with it. Add to that a millionaire husband and the fact that she is a trophy wife with ten years on the clock, and you've got someone who doesn't want anything to do with a younger woman. Especially not a blonde with attitude.' He paused before adding deliberately, 'Not to mention a figure that stops traffic.'

Nicky winced, just as he had expected. Just as she always did when anyone mentioned her looks. Martin pushed home his advantage.

'Compared with Mrs Lazenby, Esteban is a pussy cat.'

Nicky gave him an incredulous look. He laughed.

'Well, OK, maybe not a pussy cat. But he's not stupid and he's not jealous of you. And he has got a genuine problem.' He added in a wheedling tone, 'Just your sort of problem, in fact.'

Nicky could hardly deny that.

'And he wants you to deal with it personally.'

Nicky grimaced.

'You and no one else. You obviously impressed him.'

'I made him spitting mad,' corrected Nicky.

'Well, that makes two of you, doesn't it?'

Before she could answer, Martin leaned forward and studied her earnestly.

'Look, Nick, you know how I'm placed, with the exhibition and everything. I can't afford the time to go haring off to Cornwall. I'm sorry Esteban Tremain rubs your fur up the wrong way but you've just got to be professional about it.'

Nicky's jaw jutted dangerously. 'Or?' she said in a soft voice.

Martin closed his eyes. 'Nick, don't be difficult—'

'Will you give me the sack if I refuse to go?'

His eyes flew open. 'Of course not.'

'Then I refuse,' she said triumphantly.

Martin did not laugh. 'I won't need to give you the sack,' he said grimly. 'If Tremain doesn't pay his account by the end of the month the bank will probably foreclose. Then we're all out of a job.'

Nicky sat down hard. 'What?'

'I've let it get out of hand,' Martin admitted.

He stood up and thrust his hands into his pockets. He began to prowl round the room.

'My accountant tells me I've spent too much time marketing and not enough collecting the debts. To be honest, we probably shouldn't have taken a stand at the exhibition. But by the time I realised how bad things were it was too late to cancel without paying up. So I thought, What the hell?'

Nicky shut her eyes. It was all too horribly familiar. It was what her father had said all through her hand-to-mouth childhood. She had never thought to hear it from steady, sensible Martin, even though he was a long-standing friend of her ramshackle family.

'You're more like my father than I thought,' she said involuntarily.

Martin had the grace to look ashamed. But he did not back down.

Nicky watched him. She felt numb. 'I knew there was something wrong. But I had no idea it was this bad.'

'It wasn't. It's all gone wrong in the last six weeks. To be honest, I was relying on Tremain settling his account to keep going until I can put in a bill to Hambeldons.' He looked at her helplessly.

Nicky knew that look. It was just how her mother used to look when they landed on the next Caribbean island without money or stores and her father began declaring loudly that nothing would induce him to take another tourist out fishing. And Nicky knew she would do just the same now as she had then.

She swallowed. She could feel the volcano heaving under her feet, she thought.

'All right,' she said with deep reluctance. 'Leave it to me.'

Martin cheered up at once. The others were unsurprised by Nicky's decision when she was heard to telephone Esteban's secretary for route instructions and a key. They were even envious.

'He looks lonely,' sighed Sally.

'Lonely!' muttered Nicky, scornful.

'He has never met a woman to thaw his heart,' Sally went on, oblivious. She spent a lot of her time reading the stories in the magazines where Springdown Kitchens advertised. 'Don't you agree, Nicky?'

Nicky was cynical. 'I should think he's found several and returned them all to store,' she said unwisely.

Caroline laughed. 'You are so right,' she agreed. 'The shelf life of an Esteban Tremain squeeze is about six months, they say.' She added wickedly, 'That should give you a fun Christmas, Nicky.'

'He won't be there,' Nicky said hurriedly. 'I double-checked with his secretary. She says he's in London all week. As long as I'm away before Friday night, I don't have to see Esteban Tremain at all.'

It was a long drive. Normally Nicky liked driving but on this occasion it gave her too much time to think. Alone in the car with a ribbon of motorway unfolding in front of her and recipes for a bonfire-night party on the radio, her mind slipped treacherously sideways.

Why did Esteban Tremain have this effect on her? She knew nothing about the man, after all. Just that slightly spiky article, a couple of personal encounters—that slow, dispassionate assessment—the note in his voice when he'd called her a blonde. And he smelled like the sea.

She could not suppress her involuntary shiver of awareness as she remembered that. There was something about him that set all her warning antennae on full alert.

Impatiently she leaned forward and twiddled the radio dial until she found some music with a cheerful beat. She moved her shoulders to it, trying to relax. Trying to remember how to relax. Trying to remember that some people actually wanted to be blonde.

She flicked her hand through her hair. For once, knowing she was going to be alone, she had left it loose.

'Why don't you dye your hair, if you hate it so much?' one of her friends had said impatiently, when she was complaining about the blonde image.

Well, you could dye out the golden fairness, Nicky thought now. There was not much you could do about an hourglass figure and long, slim legs, unless you wanted to diet yourself into ill health. Her dislike of her looks had not yet taken her that far.

So she contented herself with wearing dark long-line jackets that disguised her remarkable figure and pulling her hair back into severe styles. Even so, it did not always work. She had learned to dread that speculative stare, as a man suddenly discovered her looks under the businesslike surface. It was too horribly reminiscent...

The car had speeded up as the memories approached. Nicky shook herself and made herself slow down.

These days she had almost forgotten that crippling sense of wanting to run until she disappeared into the horizon. Almost. Until someone like Esteban Tremain called her a blonde in *that* tone of voice.

Again Andrew's words came back to her. 'Find the guy. Get him out of your system. Or you'll never be free.'

It was getting dark. Nicky shivered. The memories of the dark were worst of all.

She left the motorway at the next exit. She found a small inn and a fire and company. For a while the memories receded.

But in the end she had to leave the friendly landlord and his wife and go up to the pretty chintz hung bedroom alone. After getting ready for bed Nicky went to the window and looked out. In this country village you could see the stars. They were more brilliant than they were in London but even so they did not compare with the jewelled coverlet of the Caribbean.

Nicky closed her eyes in anguish. No, she was not going to banish the memory tonight. She knew what that meant. No sleep until she faced it.

She sank into an armchair and tipped her head back. She let memory do its work…

CHAPTER THREE

IT WAS one of the worst times on the ramshackle Piper boat.

Oh, they were always short of money, of course, but Margaret Piper usually kept a small secret store for emergencies. This time, when she went to it, there was nothing there. Leon had found it and spent the contents. He did not even know where it had gone. Money, as he said charmingly when she challenged him, just trickled through his fingers. Money, he added, was not important.

It was one of the few times Nicky remembered seeing her mother angry with him. Not only angry but hopeless.

'I was saving that to buy Nicky a birthday present,' she heard her mother shout. 'She's sixteen next month and she hasn't even got a *skirt*.'

There was not enough money to pay the mooring fee in the small island harbour, of course. They had to drop anchor off an isolated beach, out of town, and forage for food and water. Margaret tore her arm on an acacia bush and began to cry. When Leon put his arm round her, she twitched him away, turning her shoulder so that Ben and Nicky should not see her tears.

Ben did not. But Nicky, maturing fast and increasingly aware of the strains that their itinerant life imposed on her mother, saw all too clearly. It was then that she decided to go to town.

She ignored the scratches on her bare brown legs. She ignored the fact that her old shorts and shirt had shrunk as well as faded in the wash. If, as her very own Nemesis later accused, she looked like a voluptuous Cleopatra in urchin's clothing, Nicky did not know it. All she knew was that she must do something to take that look of despair off her mother's face. Anything.

There would be work at one of the cafés on the main drag or the marina, Nicky thought. She had grown experienced in the finding of casual work on the islands. Even if they did not pay her until the end of the week—which was all too likely—she should be able to beg some food from them at the end of the evening.

Well, she got the food all right. And a lot more than she had bargained for. Or than she was equipped to deal with.

There was no work at any of the cafés. But a harassed woman laden with gaping grocery bags stopped her as she came out of the Golden Lobster.

'You looking for a job, kid?'

Nicky nodded.

'I'm cooking for a party on the *Calico Jane*. I could do with another pair of hands. Just for tonight. Fifty dollars in your hand.'

To Nicky it was a fortune. More than that, it was a lifeline. But she was clear-headed enough to remember that casual labour didn't have guaranteed hours. By the time she got off work tonight the shops could all be shut.

'Fifty dollars and the left-overs,' she said firmly.

The woman laughed. 'No way. This lot are on vintage champagne. You're not waltzing off with two-hundred-dollar bottles of wine.'

Nicky lifted her chin. 'No alcohol. Food. I want bread and salad and meat. Oh, and some milk.'

Her prospective employer stared. Then she shrugged, to the imminent danger of her grocery purchases.

'If that's what you want. Now take this damned bag and let's get going.'

Nicky did.

The *Calico Jane* was in the luxury class. Anyone who chartered her had to be well off. Nicky was used to that. There were plenty of the seriously rich who moored yachts on one Caribbean island or another. She and Ben had crewed for several of them.

But she had never seen anything like the party that greeted her as she climbed aboard *Calico Jane* in Ruth Demarco's wake. From their vintage champagne to their caviare snacks, they were behaving as if they had money to burn. They were also surprisingly young.

'More money than brains,' said Ruth briefly, retrieving three empty champagne bottles as she led the way to the galley.

'Who on earth are they?' asked Nicky, her head full of wild rumours about the Hollywood brat pack.

'New York money brokers, mainly. The guy who chartered the boat is OK but he's having dinner with some serious sailors tonight, so it's just the flotsam.' Ruth was clearly not impressed. 'Pushing the good life to the limit. Watch out for Piers. He's got more arms than an octopus.'

Nicky found out the truth of that.

It was much later. The party was over. Ruth was bagging up the last of the trash. She sent Nicky on deck to collect any remaining plates and glasses before she sent her home. The left-overs were already packed into a grocery sack and waiting for her on the countertop.

It was three in the morning and Nicky's eyes were closing. Which must have been why she did not see Piers Lane until it was too late. There were plenty of lights on deck. She should have seen him. But when he reached out and took her by the wrist Nicky nearly leaped out of her skin.

'Hey, babe.' It was not easy to slur on two words but Piers managed it. He leered up at her foggily.

Nicky stumbled. She had thought all three of the men sprawled on deck were asleep or too drunk to move. But there was a strength in Piers Lane's grip which told her exactly how wrong she had been.

She took rapid stock. The other bodies were stirring too, beginning to look interested and not very kind.

Suppressing alarm, she said in a neutral voice, 'Is there something you want, sir?'

Piers grinned and told her exactly what he wanted. In the light of her parents' philosophical commitment to freedom, Nicky was used to taking care of herself, young though she was. She reviewed the situation rapidly and decided to play down the drama.

'Maybe another time,' she said with a meaningless smile. 'I've got to clear up now.'

She pulled at his restraining hand. For a moment, his grip relaxed and she thought she would get away with it. Then one of the other revellers said something mocking in a slurred voice. Nicky did not catch the words but Piers's head reared up as if his manhood had been insulted.

He pulled at her wrist. Nicky lost her balance. And that, of course, was when the strain on the elderly buttons of her shirt became too great. Two of them shot across the deck, leaving the garment gaping. It revealed a bra that no self-respecting girl would have been seen dead in: yellow from much washing and three sizes too small.

There was an astonished silence. Piers stared at her rounded breasts under their inadequate covering. His eyes popped. Then all three of the men began to crow with glee.

'All *right*,' Piers said enthusiastically.

He pulled her down on top of him. Nicky was not experienced enough to curb her alarm in a situation like this. She let out a yell for Ruth that must have been heard all round the marina. She also kicked him hard.

She was wearing battered deck shoes, hardly younger than her blouse, so she did not make much impact. But she startled him enough to make him loosen his grip on her wrist. She twisted away, falling to her knees in her urgency to get away from him.

That was when the others decided to join in. They both jumped up. One of them hauled her to her feet but, instead of letting her go, he pushed her back against the side of the boat and knelt down in front of her, pretending to take a photograph with an imaginary camera.

'Nice!' he said, grinning.

In an anguish of embarrassment, Nicky hated them all.

Piers struggled to his feet and lurched towards her, brushing the pretend photographer out of the way, announcing, 'I saw her first.'

'Stop this,' said Nicky.

They did not hear her. Behind them she caught sight of Ruth's head appearing at the top of the companionway. The woman gave the little tableau one horrified look and darted away over the side.

Nicky had no time to call her because Piers and his friends were circling, like pre-school children round the class outsider. They were laughing drunkenly. It was as if they were playing a game and had not noticed that she did not want to join in.

She was afraid. But she was also furious. She backed up against the side of the boat and yelled hard enough to make them blink. And pause.

Her cry for help was answered.

There was a sound of running feet, an angry exclamation, then a thud which shook the deck as an athletic body vaulted lightly on to the boat.

Nicky's tormentors were confused. They turned to see what was happening. Seizing her chance, Nicky ducked and made a bolt for freedom.

She cannoned straight into a muscular body travelling just as fast in the opposite direction. Nicky reeled. Strong hands shot out to steady her but it was too late. She fell at his feet in an inelegant sprawl.

'What the *hell* is going on?' There was a force of anger in the cool voice that made the decks thrum.

'Steve?' Piers was blearily pleased to see the newcomer. He had clearly not picked up the wild anger that Nicky heard. 'Now for some fun, *mi amigo*.'

'What is this?' Even the surface of his voice was not so cool now.

Piers picked up the anger this time. He blinked, injured.

'Party time, *compadre*.'

'You call this is a *party*?' The irony was savage.

They shuffled, sobering. The pretend photographer began to back away. Only Piers threw his arms wide and gave a shout of drunken laughter.

Nicky was getting her breath back. She looked up at Steve through the curtain of her tumbled hair. Unlike the others in their bright Hawaiian shirts, he wore the minimum—brief shorts, bare chest, bare feet. He was also wearing glasses with reactive lenses. In the light of the bright lanterns on deck, they had darkened to an opaque cinder colour, making it look as if the eye sockets were empty. He looked muscular, competent and—as the eyes behind the reflecting visor brushed Nicky's semi-clad body for an electric moment—furious. Nicky's heart gave an unaccountable jolt.

'Where did she—' Steve nodded at Nicky's prone form without bothering to look at her again '—come from?'

Nicky went cold. Suddenly she was acutely aware of her sprawled length of tanned leg, torn clothes, and bare shoulder where the disreputable shirt had twisted half off her as she fell.

It was crazy! By *not* looking at her the man called Steve was making her more self-conscious than the other idiots had done when they'd leered.

She writhed inwardly, hating herself. Hating them. But then her pride kicked in and she jumped to her feet.

'Ruth took me on to help out for the evening.'

She suddenly realised that Ruth was there, hovering at a distance behind Steve. She must have gone to fetch him, Nicky realised. That made her feel worse, knowing that he had been summoned to defend her. And he had: and then he could not bear to look at her. Paradoxically, it fanned her temper to white heat.

'Waitressing and washing up was what I signed on for,'

she snarled. 'Not—' she directed a glance at Piers with loathing '—wrestling.'

Steve still did not look at her. His mouth tightened.

'It sounds like you should have asked,' he told Piers curtly.

Piers looked hurt. 'It was just a bit of fun.'

Nicky looked at him incredulously. 'Not for me it wasn't.'

Both Piers and Steve ignored her.

Steve, whoever he was, said wearily, 'Don't you get enough of that at home?'

Piers grinned. 'Can't get enough of it anywhere, old buddy. Why the disapproval? *Señoritas* fall over themselves for that Latin charm. You've had your share.'

'Not of unwilling adolescents,' snapped Steve, goaded.

'Adolescents?' Piers looked blank.

Steve looked at Nicky—briefly but at least he was acknowledging that she was there and had a voice. 'How old are you?' he demanded grimly.

'Nearly sixteen.'

He looked round the group scornfully.

It startled them. Even Piers looked uneasy.

Steve pressed the point home.

'See? She isn't just dressed like your fantasy of a school-girl. She *is* a schoolgirl.'

Piers was taken aback. It made him truculent. 'A bloody well-developed schoolgirl,' he muttered.

Nicky flinched and crossed her arms across her breasts. And found that she had forgotten how wide her shirt was gaping. She grabbed it closed, feeling the colour flood up. Not just into her face—her whole body felt as if it was burning with humiliation. She shook her hair forward, knowing that her eyes were filling with tears and there was not a thing she could do about it.

And that, of course, was the moment that Steve turned his attention full on her at last. Nicky could have screamed. She could not even dash the tears away, with both hands hauling her ruined shirt closed.

He watched her for a tense moment. Then he ripped off his glasses and said abruptly, 'Where do you live?'

Nicky swallowed a large lump in her throat. 'On a boat.'

'Here? In the marina?'

The lump was too big to swallow twice. Nicky shook her head.

His voice gentled, though he still looked as if he could barely contain his anger. 'In town?'

She shook her head again. He was obscurely different from the others. Older somehow. Certainly tougher. They were a little afraid of him, she thought. It came to her that she ought to be afraid of him too. And she wasn't.

The thought was so astounding that she stopped hiding behind her hair and stared full at him. His eyes narrowed.

'You mean it's a drive to get you home.'

His reluctance was palpable. Nicky flushed even harder. Pride came to her aid. Her chin rose.

'You don't have to do that,' she said in a cool little voice. 'I walked into town. I can walk back.'

'Not alone, you don't,' Steve told her.

He put his glasses on and pushed them up his nose with one forefinger. It was quite final.

Nicky was genuinely outraged. 'You can't stop me.'

In the act of turning away, he paused.

'You,' he said evenly, 'don't get a vote. You may look like Cleopatra on one of her more voluptuous days, but it's the urchin's clothing that tells the true story, isn't it? You've just admitted it.'

Nicky was lost. 'What do you mean?'

'Fifteen-year-olds do what they're told,' he told her. 'Come on.' He turned back to the gangway, motioning her to follow him with an abrupt gesture. 'Let's get going.'

Ruth met them at the top of the companionway. She pushed Nicky's grocery bag at her.

'Steve will take care of you,' she said loudly, and touched Nicky's shoulder in silent encouragement.

Steve flashed her an ironic look over his shoulder.

'All right, Ruth. Point taken.'

Gee, thanks, thought Nicky, confused and annoyed. She stamped after him bad-temperedly.

Steve looked down at her. 'Now what's wrong?'

'I wasn't doing so badly at taking care of myself,' she muttered. 'In spite of the Neanderthal kindergarten back there.'

He gave a snort of surprised laughter. But he said, 'Just as well Ruth came to get me, though.'

She hunched her shoulders sulkily and followed without another word.

The marina was modern and well lit. Disastrously well lit. About to help Nicky into the Jeep, Steve unthinkingly took the grocery sack from her. Before she could catch them, the edges of her shirt blew wide in the night breeze. Which left him staring straight down onto her inadequately covered breasts. Floodlit.

She forgot her sulks. 'Oh, no!' she shouted, scarlet-faced.

He froze. The light-sensitive glasses hid his eyes but his mouth looked as if it was etched in stone. Nicky made a small sound of total despair and shut her eyes.

'I guess I'm going to have to find you something to wear,' he said ruefully. 'Or neither of us is going to be able to concentrate.'

Nicky set her teeth and did not answer. He went to the back of the Jeep and began to rummage. She opened her eyes cautiously. The marina was deserted. Heavily rhythmic music blared intermittently down the breeze from one of the beach cafés beyond. But there was no one to be seen on the boats or the brightly lit waterfront. Just Nicky and the man she ought to think of as her rescuer—and was rapidly coming to hate.

She hauled the shirt round her so hard she heard one of the seams rip. Great. That cut her wardrobe of wearable shirts down to two.

Steve straightened and came back to her. He held out a

rag that smelled noticeably of gasoline. Nicky took it reluctantly.

'Put it on.'

She hesitated.

He was impatient. 'It's not Chanel but it will keep the cold out.' And, as she still hesitated, he added deliberately, 'You're not getting into the Jeep until you do.'

Nicky pulled it on without a word.

He opened the passenger door for her but he did not help her to climb up. She tied the corners of the flapping shirt at her waist and then hauled herself up into the Jeep. She did not look at him. Once up, she sat as far away from the driver's seat as she could manage.

He got in and drove out of the marina, handling the Jeep with the careless ease of long practice. Nicky watched his hands on the wheel. They were long-fingered and powerful. She saw a man who was so used to being in control of the machinery of his life that he did not even think about it. She shuddered a little and drew even further into her corner.

Except for a curt request for directions, Steve did not speak at all. Nicky was equally silent. They met nothing on the road. Once away from the marina, there were no lights at all, just the black funnel of the road in their headlights, and the murmuring shadow of the sea to their right. Nicky turned her head towards it and tried not to think about the silent man beside her.

It was not easy. She had only to turn her head the slightest and she could see those confident hands. For some reason, they filled her with a strange excitement. In fact the man called Steve made her feel uncertain in a way she had never experienced before.

It was quite different from the black panic she had felt on the boat. It was half discomfort, half anticipation. Like the evening breeze on sun blasted skin, it was a shock and a pleasure at the same time. It kept her on the edge of her seat.

Above all, she realised, she wanted him to stop the Jeep. She wanted—no, she *needed*—him to take those sure hands off the steering wheel and touch her. It seemed all wrong that he had not touched her already. He had rescued her, protected her, delivered her home—well, nearly—and yet he stayed at a stranger's distance.

Well, he is a stranger, Nicky told herself.

She took herself to task. She was shaky, jittery, not herself. The events of the evening had taken a toll of her common sense. Just because he had long, beautiful hands and had saved her from an awkward situation that was no reason to feel they were no longer strangers.

But she was so distracted by her wayward thoughts that she almost missed the turning.

'Here,' she said, so sharply that he had to brake hard before swinging the Jeep onto the beach track.

The lurch sent her sideways. Their shoulders touched. Nicky felt her body stop, as if suddenly all its systems had gone on hold, waiting for new instructions. Then her insides seemed to start shivering, as if she had been drenched in ice.

Steve did not appear to notice anything. He took the Jeep down through the bushes until the beach opened out ahead. He stopped and cut the lights. In front of them the dark sea stretched and rolled like a lazy animal. The sky was frosted with stars. Nicky held her breath.

'Here?'

Was it her imagination or did his voice sound strained?

'The boat is moored further up.'

'Oh.' He did not move. Then he said, 'Have you got a torch?'

Yes, definitely strained.

'No.'

'There's one in the back. I'll get it and walk you down the beach.'

But still he did not move. Nicky detected reluctance. She was consumed with humiliation.

'There's no need. It's bright enough to see.'

'Don't be prickly. I'd prefer to walk you home.'

Nicky shrugged. But she could not resist another sideways

look at those powerful hands. She found he was gripping the wheel as if it were a life belt. It astonished her.

'Are you all right?' she said involuntarily.

She saw his throat move as he swallowed. She wished, passionately, that she could see his eyes. But it was dark. Anyway, the mirrored lenses stayed firmly in place.

'I'm fine. Come on. Let's get you home.'

He got the torch—a square box of a thing that lit up the beach like the car's headlights. He also pulled on some deck shoes. Nicky, who knew that sea urchins could lurk in the powdery sand, approved this forethought. It showed that his air of competence was not all window-dressing.

He hefted her grocery sack onto one hip and hooked the light onto his belt. Then he motioned her to lead the way.

She could feel his eyes on her as she plodded through the sand. She slipped several times. He never put out a hand to help her, though once she thought he was on the point of it and curbed his instinct.

So she was not wrong, Nicky thought wretchedly. He was not touching her quite deliberately. What a nuisance he must think her. What a clumsy, useless nuisance. The back of her neck felt hot with embarrassment.

At last she stopped.

'Here.'

He came close beside her and turned, raking the sea with the flashlight. The beam caught the lines of the *Pompilia*. Steve drew in a breath as if the sight surprised him.

'So there really is a boat,' he said, confirming it.

'Of course.' Nicky was bewildered. 'What did you think?'

The glasses turned towards her briefly. 'Frankly, I thought you were probably sleeping rough. On the beach.'

Nicky gasped. 'But that's against the law.'

'So?'

She rounded on him. 'What do you think I am?' she cried hotly.

There was an odd silence. She could hear the blood pounding in her ears. But the sounds of the night, the sea and the busy cicadas, were suddenly muted. Nicky thought suddenly, I wish I hadn't said that.

Then Steve said, very evenly, 'You wouldn't want to know.'

Nicky froze. She wanted to move way, pelt for the water and swim out to the *Pompilia* and never see him again. She wanted not to move a muscle until he touched her. Her mouth parted. The moment stretched out for ever. She wanted him to take her in his arms...

Shocked, she thought, Have I gone *crazy*?

The picture in her mind was so vivid—and so utterly beyond her experience—that she flinched away from it, physically. Steve felt the movement and put out a hand to save her at last. But it was too late. He was closer than she realised and she stumbled against him.

He gave a grunt of shock and dropped the groceries. Worse, the flashlight shot off his belt. It landed squashily in the sand and the light went out.

The stars were suddenly a lot closer. He was breathing hard as if she had really hurt him.

'Oh, I'm sorry,' Nicky cried, horrified.

'It's all right.' It sounded as if he was saying it between his teeth. He must be furious with her.

'I didn't mean to—'

'It's all *right*.'

She dropped to her knees, reaching for the groceries, the flashlight, apologising feverishly. Only then she scraped her hand along the leaf of a hidden clump of sea clover and recoiled, with a sharp exclamation.

'Ouch.'

'What is it?' he said in quick concern.

He took a hasty step forward and stumbled over her foot. It brought him down on one knee. Which meant they were both kneeling in the sand. Very close and both of them off balance.

He put out a hand to steady himself. It brushed her bare

flesh where she had knotted the shirt at her waist above her shorts. Steve went very still.

Slowly Nicky turned her head. His body was so close that she had to blink in order not to sway against him. The sense of his body's heat and strength overwhelmed her. She could see the dark shape of his head; his shoulders against the sky; hear his breathing. Hear when, just for an electric moment, it stopped.

She leaned forward and kissed him quickly, clumsily.

He started breathing again, dragging the air from the very bottom of his lungs in harsh gasps.

'Don't—' It sounded strangled.

But Nicky was beyond thought, shaking with need. This was new. It was dangerous. She knew it but she did not care. She just wanted Steve to take charge again and lead her into the new place that she dimly realised she had been making towards since she'd first seen him this evening.

He knows it too, she thought, listening to his harsh breathing. He knew it before I did.

She wound her arms round his neck and pressed trembling lips to the base of his throat. He felt like rock.

'I tried.' It sounded as if it was torn out of him.

Then, as if he could not help himself, he slammed an arm round her and hauled her against him. Their bodies fused along their whole length. Suddenly Nicky knew, beyond question, exactly how aroused he was. Her indrawn breath was half shock, half wonder.

Steve's palm was warm at the naked skin of her waist. He tipped her gently down on to the sand. She went, with a sigh of deliverance. It all felt inevitable, somehow.

After that, it happened in slow motion, Nicky thought afterwards. He seemed bent on learning her body, touch by exquisite touch. She felt her clothes pushed aside; the roughness of his unshaven cheek against her tender breast, his breath on her skin. This was utterly new to her. But she felt no fear. Only a deep, wondering delight. Shyly she ran her hand down his beautiful naked spine.

And then his touch was no longer a slow revelation but urgent, urgent...

As she remembered, Nicky's nails dug into her palms. This was the point when she used to exclaim aloud, jump up, walk away, do anything to block out what happened next. But these days she knew better. Maturity came from taking responsibility for your mistakes. And accepting the consequences.

And she had been responsible. There was no doubt about that. Carried away on a tide of feeling, she had twined round him like a vine. Met his every demand eagerly. Made demands of her own that, inexperienced as she was, she had never dreamed of before.

Until, twisting to get rid of their last scraps of clothing, Steve had given a yelp of pain.

'What?' Nicky was dazed. 'What did I do?'

'Nothing.' He pulled away from her, nursing his foot as he rocked with pain. 'I stubbed my toe.'

She gave a soft laugh, nuzzling his shoulder. 'Shall I kiss it better?'

'*No.*'

He stopped rocking. Nicky said his name voicelessly, her lips moving against the warm skin of his shoulder. But he did not take her in his arms again. Instead he drew back so sharply that she fell forward and had to put out hands into the powdery sand to save herself. He looked down at her crouching form. Against the starry sky, she saw him shake his head slowly.

'What am I doing?' It was a ragged whisper. He was not talking to her.

Nicky sat up and pushed the flying hair off her face. 'We,' she whispered. She reached up to him. 'We are doing.'

He caught her wrists, pushing her away so hard that she fell back, flat in the sand. He bent over her, holding her arms captive behind her head.

'All right, I admit it. You're dynamite. But I—will—not.' He sounded as if he was in pain.

Nicky did not understand. She wrapped a leg round him, murmuring. She felt him shudder deeply.

He drew a long breath. 'I can control this. I *can* control this.'

And even then she did not understand.

'Steve,' she whispered longingly. It was the first time she had dared to use his name.

And the last. He flung himself away from her as if she had spat poison.

'I must be out of my mind.'

Nicky did not move. Although he had released her hands she just lay as he had left her, staring. She felt as if she had been turned to stone. Her voice would not work.

'This is as far as I go.' His voice was ragged.

Even in the darkness, she could see that Steve's chest was rising and falling as if he had run a hard race. He leaped to his feet. Nicky had no doubt at all that he meant every word. Bewildered, she sat up.

He took three rapid steps away and stumbled over one of Ruth's foil-wrapped packets of food. He picked it up, astonished, turning it over in his hands as if he thought it was a bomb.

Nicky said in self-defence—as if it mattered, *now*—'Ruth said I could take home what was left after the party.' She sounded defensive, even sullen. And—to her fury—*young*.

Steve looked at the packet again. He slapped it down on to the sand beside her. There was distaste in every line of him.

'There. Take your pickings and—'

Another thought occurred to him. He paused.

Then he said in tones of despair, 'Were you paid this evening?'

Nicky had forgotten about payment. Now, constrained and wretched, she shook her head.

She thought he said, 'Oh, God.'

He rummaged in his pocket and brought out a fold of notes. Without counting them, he thrust the wad down at her. Nicky pushed it away.

He drew in several lungfuls of air. Then, carefully not touching her, he said in a gentler tone, 'Can you afford to refuse?'

Nicky put her hands over her face.

He gave an exasperated sigh and dropped the money on the sand beside her.

'Look, this evening— You shouldn't— Oh, *hell.*'

Nicky struggled to her feet. She bent and picked up the money, stuffing it into the grocery sack along with such packets of food as she could find. In the darkness her hands unexpectedly found a cylindrical object, hard—was it glass? A jar, of some sort? Enlightenment dawned. The coffee? He must have stubbed his toe on the jar of instant coffee Ruth had given her.

Nicky could not help herself. It was hysteria, of course. She began to laugh. For a terrible moment she thought she would never be able to stop.

Steve stopped dead. She saw him turn his head. The black shadow watched her, oddly menacing in its gathering stillness.

Eventually he said, 'So at least I've given you a good laugh.'

Nicky's laughter died abruptly as he took three steps forward. Nicky gave ground.

Under the jewelled sky he looked as tall as a tree. A powerful arm shot out. No dragging her against his aroused body this time. He held her at arm's length, his teeth a flash of white in a mirthless smile.

'I should have let Piers get on with it, shouldn't I?' he flung at her. 'It was a really successful production: schoolgirl meets dirty dog. I suppose you were both enjoying it. I should never have interfered.'

Nicky did not understand. She was shaking. 'N-n-no—'

'That was what you really wanted, wasn't it? No woman dresses like that unless she intends a man to strip her.'

He pulled her against him at last. Anger made him clumsy. The kiss was an assault. No semblance of seduction now.

The urgency was still there but even Nicky, inexperienced and humiliated, could recognise rage. She struggled but he was too strong for her. He held her, devoured her, until her resistance broke and she stood passive in his arms.

When he let her go she was sobbing inwardly. But some remnant of pride would not let him know.

She said harshly, 'If you don't go now I shall scream.'

'Very dramatic.' He sounded furious. 'Who would come?'

Suddenly her lip was trembling, her voice thick. 'M-my parents.'

'Your parents?' He was thunderstruck. 'You mean—' His hands on her shoulders gripped like a vice. 'You really are fifteen after all.'

'S-sixteen the week after next.'

Through the hands on her shoulders she felt his whole body flinch.

'Oh, my God,' he said quietly.

Nicky threw the glass jar at him. She was trembling. It was an anger as great as his own, she assured herself.

He caught the jar one-handed and put it down in the sand with exaggerated care. It felt like an insult.

'Go away,' she shouted.

As if on cue a light appeared on the deck of the boat. Then another.

'Looks like your fine protective parents are lining up,' Steve said cynically. 'Better late than never, I guess. Tell them they're lucky it wasn't too late.'

He turned on his heel.

'I hate you,' Nicky shouted after him.

But he kept on walking.

When her parents came to get her she was alone on the beach. Leon was inclined to be amused that his cautious daughter had given her parents cause for concern at last.

Margaret was not. One look at Nicky's face in the torchlight and she told Leon to shut up. It was so unusual that he did.

Nicky let them take her back to the *Pompilia* as if she were in a dream. But when she went to bed she could not sleep. She curled up in a tight, tight ball, closed her eyes hard and willed herself to forget everything: his savage contempt, that kiss, everything that, heaven help her, she had *wanted*. It did not work.

In the morning she was hollow-eyed enough to disturb even her father. Her mother, who by then had found the roll of notes in the grocery sack, was white with concern.

'Oh, Nicky, what have you done?'

Nicky flinched away and would not tell.

'We must leave this horrible island,' Margaret told Leon with unheard-of resolution.

He was so surprised that he did not argue. Only they needed to get supplies, didn't they? So before they left the island completely he sailed the boat round the coast.

When they got to town they found that it was market day. There was a general air of carnival about the quayside. Tourists were moving through the crowd, snapping their fingers to the beat of the bands and laughing. And the first person Nicky saw was Piers.

He was looking very sorry for himself. Last night's excesses had clearly taken their toll. Resisting the rhythm, he was walking slowly with the careful air of a man who was not quite sure whether he was going to be sick or not. He did not take his eyes off the cobbled road. If Nicky had not stopped dead, so that Margaret bumped into her, Piers would probably not even have noticed her.

But she did. Margaret, behind Nicky, did not see the look of horror on her face. But Piers did. He flushed; then looked angry.

He turned and called over his shoulder, 'Hey, Steve, the blonde totty is back.'

Nicky could not move.

'Darling, do get a move on. We haven't got all day,' said Margaret, oblivious.

Then, strolling among the vendors of red snapper and butter squash and sugar apples, appeared the man of her nightmares. This morning he was wearing crisp khaki shorts and an olive shirt. He still hadn't taken off those beastly dark-lensed glasses, Nicky saw, hating them and him.

He stopped beside Piers; looked across the quay; saw her. Nicky made a strangled sound. Steve went very still.

The air was full of cheerful talk. There was the inevitable bouncy beat of the local band, playing just ten steps away along the quay. Behind both, the sea slapped steadily against the dock. The traders had taken up places under bright umbrellas, their wares equally fluorescent. It was one great big street party. Nicky was the only person not lazy and happy.

She thought she would hate carnivals for the rest of her life.

Steve's eyes were hidden, of course. But as far as Nicky could see his expression did not change when he saw her. After the briefest pause, he nodded, unsmiling.

Margaret realised something was wrong. She stopped fussing with her shopping list.

'Darling, do you know those men?' she asked under her breath.

Nicky could not speak. She shook her head, not taking her eyes off Steve's unresponsive face. He hesitated; then, after a quick look at Margaret, he came over to them.

'Good morning. No ill effects from your late night?' he asked lightly.

Nicky stood as still as stone. Margaret's eyes sharpened suspiciously.

'So it was you my daughter was with last night.'

Steve said hastily, 'She was with all of us. We had a party on board. She helped out in the galley.' He gave her a kind, indifferent smile. 'Very well. We were grateful.'

Nicky said nothing. She would remember those blanked eyes for the rest of her life.

'Oh,' said Margaret, her worry dissipating.

Nicky had helped out on plenty of boats and never come to harm. And, while Margaret didn't like the look of the other boy, people who had hangovers could not be expected to be at their best. Steve, whoever he was, was clearly mature and responsible. Too mature and responsible to do to Nicky what she had been more than half afraid of this morning.

She gave him a wide, relieved smile. 'I'm glad—'

Which was the moment at which Piers took a hand.

'Going to come and play again tonight, sweetheart?'

Steve silenced him with a savage expletive. Piers grinned.

'Hell, don't be a killjoy. I really dig that trick with the buttons—' And he flapped his shirt in a pantomime gesture, horribly explicit.

There was a terrible moment when nobody said anything. It was like waiting for the headland you were standing on to crumble, Nicky thought. Her heart beat with agonising hammer blows. Her eyes turned to Steve, helplessly.

'I said, shut *up*,' he flung at Piers furiously.

It was too late. Nicky did not wait for any more. She knew her mother was staring. She could not bear it. Pushing past them blindly, she took off into the covered market, running as if the whole world were after her.

She had to go back in the end, of course. Shamefaced, she slipped back on to the boat, half hoping, half fearing that Margaret would demand an explanation. But Margaret had talked to Steve and drawn her own conclusions. Now she was struggling with remorse.

'Darling, I just hadn't realised how you were growing up. I'm so sorry. I should never have let it come to this. We are going to buy you some new clothes the moment we get to Kingston.'

'New *clothes*?'

Nicky could hardly believe her ears. Her life was shattered and her mother was worried about her wardrobe? Margaret looked uncomfortable.

'You really have outgrown everything. *We* know that's

why your clothes are a bit skimpy. But other people—well, men—can get the wrong idea.'

Nicky whitened.

'It's not your fault,' Margaret said hastily. 'But, my point is, it's not theirs either. You do look—'

'A blonde totty,' said Nicky, tightly.

Margaret laughed. 'Well, a bit, darling.'

'I won't ever again.'

And she had not.

Ten years later, Nicky found she was pulling her dressing gown round her so hard that her fingers were white with the effort. Deliberately she relaxed her clenched hands. She was holding her breath as if bracing herself against an expected pain.

But it was not painful any more, she assured herself. At least, it shouldn't be. She had dealt with it, put it behind her. No matter what Andrew said, she could handle it. She had got up and gone to work the next day, got her life back on track, picked herself up ready to go on again. Hadn't she?

She let out a slow, ragged breath.

Well, yes, she had. Until Martin had told her to do what Esteban Tremain wanted.

Why?

Nicky had no answer for that. Maybe it was the hint of masculine coercion. Or maybe— She did not know.

She did not take the dressing gown off when she got into bed. She told herself it was because the room was cold. It was not true. It was because she wanted the protection of heavy cloth huddled round her. As if she could take its defences into her dreams with her, Nicky thought wryly. After she had let the memories surface again, she knew exactly the sort of dream she was likely to have.

She was right. Only this time there was another man stalking through the terrible carnival. In the dream Nicky followed him along the quay. Only then the sea wall ran out and he turned to face her. It was Esteban Tremain.

CHAPTER FOUR

IT WAS late. He should have been working. Esteban looked at the papers spread out over his big desk and recognised that his concentration was shot to hell.

He stood up and moved restlessly to the window. He was gazing down on to an exclusive London private quay. But other images danced in front of his eyes so that he did not know what it was that was really disturbing him.

Francesca, of course, was appalling. He had never been in love with her but he had liked her. And when he'd found she had spilled his private life to a journalist her disloyalty had shocked him. Not that, in the end, the journalist had printed all that much. But when she'd threatened to talk about the girl from the boat he'd believed her.

A pulse started to beat in Esteban's temple. He touched irritable fingers to it.

Why did it still matter so much? By now, the girl would have forgotten, anyway. She certainly would not be the brave, vulnerable, fighting creature that had awakened something in him ten years ago. Something that Francesca and a dozen others had never managed to touch since.

Esteban looked out of the window and saw not the lights from the building reflected in the oily water, but a pale, furious face, surrounded by a mass of gold curls; lips that trembled in spite of her fierce words; legs that somehow seemed too long for her, like a young colt...

'Hold it right there,' he said to himself. Just as he had said ten years ago.

In spite of her spirited defence on the boat she had been so unsure, so *young*. Too young. Too young for the feelings she'd aroused in him. Too young, when she'd kissed him on the beach, to know how dangerous her innocent sensuality was. And far, far too young to understand the adult anger when he'd lashed out at her.

Esteban closed his eyes against that memory. It made no difference. He still saw her shocked face, that morning on the quay. As if she could not believe that anyone could be as heedlessly cruel as he had been the previous night; as if she hated him.

He'd deserved it, he thought dispassionately. In fact it had probably been a good thing for her that she had hated him. It would have helped her get over it. That was why, in the end, he had given up trying to find her, although he probably could have done if he had stuck at it.

He had thought it best to let the whole incident slip into the past. Only—it wouldn't stay there. 'Do something wicked and it stays with you,' Esteban told himself bitterly. The only reason Francesca knew about the girl was because he had told her one day when his conscience was pricking him and she seemed sympathetic.

He shook his head. Why was he thinking about things that happened so long ago? He had urgent problems sitting there on his desk. He needed to find a way to sort out his stepfather's precarious finances.

His expression darkened. There was a simple answer to Patrick's difficulties: sell some paintings. But every time Esteban suggested it Patrick just blanked out. So far Esteban had managed to subsidise Hallam. But he was already working all hours, taking every case that was offered him, and Hallam's expenses went on growing. In fact he wondered now whether the new kitchen had been a waste of money, if Patrick was going to have to sell the Hall after all.

Unexpectedly, Esteban's mouth quirked. If he had not bought the new kitchen, he would not have crossed swords with Nicola Piper. Now, that had to be worth it. In her way she had the same passionate belief in herself as his urchin Cleopatra.

He left the window and went back to his papers.

By three in the morning, his eyes were gritty with tiredness and Patrick's finances seemed, if anything, in greater turmoil than ever. Really, Esteban ought to see him; make him understand that there was no alternative to selling one of the paintings.

'Fat chance,' said Esteban aloud.

He stood up, flexing his cramped neck. What I want, he thought, is fresh air. Or, even better, a run.

He ran along the silent quay, his feet pounding in regular rhythm. In the summer the small dockside had been full of tubs of bright flowers. Now the plants were straggling and withered, waving in the strong wind off the river. There was rain in the air.

Esteban finished his circuit and hesitated for a moment outside his luxurious apartment block. He looked up. There was no way you could see the stars through the sodium lights and the blanket of London vapours. He was filled with a great longing for the sea and the cool, sharp air of Cornwall.

Well, why not? He wasn't in court for the next few days and he had no meetings he couldn't postpone. If he took his laptop computer and his modem, he could work in Hallam just as well as here. And if he talked to Patrick over several days perhaps he could convince him at last.

He yawned hugely. There was something in the back of his mind that felt like a reason not to go but he could not remember what it was. He shrugged. He would deal with the future of Hallam once and for all. It was time.

The morning chased the ghosts away. In fact Nicky began to enjoy herself, driving down country lanes in the late October sunshine with a bouncy dance tune filling the car's interior. Even when she thought she was lost, she only laughed and resolved to ask at the next village pub.

'If there is a pub between here and the end of the world,' she said aloud as the road got narrower and narrower.

By now the car doors were being scratched on both sides by autumnal blackberry bushes, their spines exposed as leaves and fruit withered. The road surface was deeply rutted, too. It felt as if no one had been down this road for months.

'Or maybe I should turn back now to the last village,' she said blithely. 'At this rate I'll be able to write the definitive Lost Guide to Cornwall.'

Only then she saw the sign. It was small and so old that she could barely make out the words. What was more it looked as if, even when it was new, it had been scrawled on a piece of bark by an amateur. The lane it indicated was no more than a rough track. But it did, indubitably, say Hallam Hall.

'Go with the flow,' said Nicky bravely.

She did. The car bounced so badly on this track that her head twice bumped the roof. Well, that would account for the damaged appliances, she thought. Shaken to pieces before they even arrived. The unkempt bushes nearly met, so that it looked as if the car was cutting its way through jungle.

'What a dump,' Nicky said.

She turned up the music, snapping her fingers to the beat defiantly. And then she saw the sea.

Nicky gasped. It was as brilliant as a tilting mirror in the October sun. She had a brief, disconcerting vision of driving straight out into the gleaming air. Then, when she had hardly got her breath back, the path dropped abruptly downhill and she saw the house.

'Oh, wonderful,' she said. 'It's not a house. It's a blasted castle. There's probably wet rot, dry rot and enough damp to short every single machine Springdown put in.'

Her diagnosis was reinforced when she stepped into a dark, panelled hall. The smell of damp and old polish smote her. Nicky made a face.

She pulled out her mobile phone and reported in.

Sally answered. 'Find it all right?'

'No problem. Hallam Hall is the only thing that stops you driving right off the cliff.'

'Is it wonderful?' Sally sounded envious.

'Bit creepy, so far. It smells like a church.'

'Ghosts?'

Nicky looked round the tapestry-hung stone walls. The sunlight did not penetrate this far.

'Dozens, I should think.'

'Will you be afraid to be there on your own?'

Nicky laughed. 'If I'm not afraid of angry plumbers, I'm not going to be seen off by any Blackbeard the Pirate Spook.'

'Oooh, you are brave. How bad does it look?'

'Haven't started yet. Have you heard any more from the client?'

Nicky could hear Sally riffling through pages of messages on her desk. 'His secretary rang to say if there is anything more you want to call her. The cleaning lady has gone to Madeira for two weeks but she should have left everything ready for you.'

Nicky shivered. 'That doesn't seem to run to putting on the central heating. Oh, well, I suppose I'll find the controls somewhere.'

'Of course you will.' Sally thought Nicky could cope with anything. 'Is it very cold?'

Nicky peered out of the leaded window. The sea was grey, the wind whipping the waves into foam.

'Yes.'

Sally moaned sympathetically. 'And you're really sure you don't mind being there on your own?'

To her private disgust, Nicky knew that she would have been a lot of happier if Martin had been at Hallam Hall too. Or even Ben. Then she had a thought and grinned.

'It beats being here with the client,' she said with feeling.

She rang off and set about unpacking the car. Then she tracked down the heating controls to a cloakroom cupboard. She turned them on. An asthmatic boiler wheezed into action without noticeable effect.

It will take for ever to heat a house this size, thought the experienced Nicky with gloom. And as for hot water! She could only pray that there was an immersion heater some-where. She began to explore the cold house.

And was astounded. The place might look like a fortress

from the outside, but inside it was pure Mediterranean paradise.

There were paintings of riotous gods and peasants in every room. On walls where there were no paintings, sculptures were set against *trompe-l'oeil* alcoves. Painted terraces were half hidden by swathes of real velvet. The whole of one wall in the high-ceilinged dining room was an olive grove, with nymphs in wafting draperies dancing through a lemon-tinged twilight.

In fact, thought Nicky grimly, she had never seen so many nymphs in all her life. Some played among trees, some dreamed by fountains, some languished on flower-strewn banks and looked frankly wanton. They were every shape and size, from tall, graceful girls with hair as loose as their draperies to the plumply luscious whose elaborate garments looked as if they had been specifically designed to fall off at the touch of a godlike hand. It all added up to a rich mixture of sun, sex and classical landscape.

Great, thought Nicky. Just what I need.

She hunched her shoulders and turned her back firmly on the laughing nymphs.

'Immersion heater,' she said. 'Work. Get moving.'

She stood up and began to make her way systematically round the kitchen. To her huge relief she found an immersion heater quite quickly. The next hurdle was to see whether it was working.

'Well, the pilot light is on,' said Nicky, trying to encourage herself.

She set out her work plan, her files, the instruction books for the appliances and the box of provisions she had brought down with her. She set out the food and looked at her schedule. First check the main fuses. Well, that was easily done.

Nicky went back to the control cupboard. Yes, there it was, clearly labelled 'power points, ground floor east wing'. The circuit breaker was still in place. She knew enough about electricity to check, just to be sure. But it did not take long to establish that the reason that the machines were not working had to lie somewhere else.

'Probably mice,' muttered Nicky as a castle-sized draft whipped round her ankles.

She went back to the kitchen and plugged in the small travelling kettle she always brought with her. She was going to need coffee.

While she was waiting for it to boil, she took critical stock. This was one of Martin's rustic kitchens, all mellow cherry wood and brass handles. It was—as far as she could see— perfectly finished. But, until Nicky had arrived and set out the tools of her trade and messed it up, it could have been in the showroom. There were absolutely no signs of an individual occupant.

If Esteban Tremain had a lady in residence, she had not left her mark on the kitchen. Nicky grimaced at the thought. Probably not surprising. No doubt she was perfectly groomed, with cool, elegant manners, and research-laboratory standards of hygiene. Not, Nicky thought wryly, someone who lost her temper at the drop of a hat and blushed when he looked at her.

'Not that it matters. Whoever he chooses is welcome to him,' Nicky said with feeling.

She worked her way through a cycle of preparing and cooking a full meal. Springdown had found it was the best way to test everything. By the time the light was failing she had established that the freezer did not work. Nor did the shining new Aga, the microwave, the kettle, the waste disposal unit or the coffee-grinder.

Judging by the delicious smells which emerged after Nicky put the pheasant casserole in to cook, however, the small gas stove had life of a sort, though neither the automatic ignition nor the timer worked. Nicky noted it carefully and sipped coffee. Suddenly the kitchen was warm, with the sort of smells a kitchen should have, and Hallam felt a friendlier place.

The preparation of an apple pie and a chocolate cake had

left her with throbbing wrists, though, because she had established that the electric mixer was not working either.
Nicky had had to cream butter and sugar and crumb flour
and fat all by hand. As a result, her hands were caked, she
had smears of flour on her face and her autumn-gold sweater
looked like army camouflage under its additions of butter and
chocolate.

'Bath,' said Nicky with resolution.

She had found only one bed made up, presumably for her
use. The bathroom next door had another immersion heater.

'Thank God,' she said devoutly, switching it on.

Her reflection in the bathroom mirror told her only too
clearly how badly she stood in need of a bath.

'You're a messy cook,' Nicky told her image.

She was feeling more cheerful by the second. The house
was getting warmer, more human, as she put her stamp on
the place.

She checked the pheasant and looked at the clock. The
bath water should be hot by now. Outside it was fully dark.
If she were really Hallam Hall's hostess, this would be the
time when she would go and have a bath and get ready for
her guests. But then if she were really Hallam Hall's hostess
she would be the cool and elegant lady she imagined.

Nicky gave an involuntary shiver, all her cheerfulness
shrivelling as the thought touched her. It was like borrowing
somebody else's life. But she needed a bath and Esteban
Tremain was safely far away in London.

So as soon as the water was hot she climbed into a bath
with claw feet and limescale deposits under the taps that
would have made a geologist swoon with envy. There was
no soap or bath preparations. Not even towels.

'Just as well I brought my own,' murmured Nicky.

But the immersion heater was efficient and the water was
blessedly hot. She sprinkled a few drops of her precious
Roman bath oil into the water and lay back in the scented
steam. Slowly, slowly, she felt the tensions of the drive and
the strange house float away. Even the unwanted memories

slipped back into the past where they belonged.

Scented steam clouded all the bathroom's Victorian mirrors. It hung in the air like aromatic fog. Nicky breathed in luxuriously. She relaxed, dreaming...

And suddenly came bolt upright, water spraying everywhere. *What if the fault was electrical after all?* Not at the mains but in the individual plugs? Why hadn't she checked at least one plug earlier?

Nicky shook her head to clear it. The mirrors were still clouded but the fog had dispersed. What was worse, she found the water had cooled. She leaped out of the tepid bath, shivering.

Hurriedly she pulled on her elderly dressing gown and thrust her feet into flip-flops. Neither was enough protection in this freezing cold pile but at least the kitchen would be warm. She ignored the cold as she dashed along the corridor. The inadequate lighting made every dark corner spooky but Nicky was too excited by her idea to notice.

Her dressing gown swung wide as she scampered down the grand staircase. Impatiently she knotted the sash. The smell wafting up from the kitchen was rich. She had better just check on the casserole before starting to look for the screwdriver.

In the kitchen she grabbed a tea-towel. She had brought several too, and just as well. In the absence of an oven glove one of them would have to serve. She opened the gleaming oven door and a warm, appetising smell rolled out. Well, at least the gas stove had not collapsed while she was in the bath.

She was easing the casserole out of the oven when the kitchen door banged open. Concentrating, she did not really notice.

Not, at least, until a voice said blankly, 'What the *hell*...?'

Only the greatest self-possession stopped Nicky from whipping round. As it was her hands tightened so hard on the casserole that she burnt herself through the imperfect insulation of the cloth. She banged the casserole down and shook her singed fingers as she turned to face him.

It was, of course, Esteban Tremain.

Nicky's heart lurched. She felt her colour rise.

'You!' she exclaimed, glaring.

Esteban blinked. He looked as if he had been miles away and had suddenly been brought back to the present with a jolt. Not, Nicky thought, a very welcome jolt. There was an unnerving silence.

Then he said, 'Nicola Piper,' on a low note of discovery.

A look of unholy appreciation dawned. Exactly the sort of look that made Nicky's hackles rise. 'What are you doing here?'

'You took the words right out of my mouth,' he drawled.

Nicky's blush deepened. She ignored it.

'You knew I was here,' she said hotly. 'Your secretary arranged it. And,' she added accusingly, 'she said you were fixed in London.'

His eyebrows twitched together.

'I was,' he said briefly. 'I changed my mind. I have business down here. Should I apologise for being in my own house?'

Nicky shifted in annoyance. It brought imminent danger to her hastily knotted sash. She felt the thing begin to slip untied and clamped the lapels of the dressing gown across her breast, flustered.

Esteban Tremain looked amused. That enraged Nicky even more. But there was nothing she could do about it. She felt rather breathless.

He let his eyes rest on the exposed vee at the top of her dressing gown. It suddenly felt incredibly bare. Involuntarily, Nicky shuddered. It infuriated her. His expression grew frankly speculative.

'You seem to have made yourself comfortable.'

That was the final straw.

'I am not comfortable,' Nicky yelled.

There was a tense pause.

Then he asked, 'Do you expect me to apologise for that too?'

Nicky took hold of her temper. It was an effort. But she was an adult, she was a professional and she was here representing Springdown. Or so she reminded herself.

'I can do without apologies. I do expect reasonable courtesy,' she said levelly.

A faint look of annoyance crossed the handsome face. 'And how have I been discourteous?'

In the way you look at me. No, she couldn't say that. It sounded too prim for words, even though it was true. And it should not have been true, thought Nicky rebelliously.

She was not fifteen any more. These days she could handle male salaciousness. Nine times out of ten it was purely for show. The moment you challenged them they backed down. And on the tenth—well, she could handle that too if she had to. Her chin rose.

'You implied that I was here for my own amusement,' she said with dignity.

One eyebrow shot up. 'Are you saying that you're here for mine?'

Her eyes flashed. 'Of course not.'

'Well, then—'

Nicky took an impetuous step forward.

'You keep complaining about your blasted kitchen,' she reminded him. 'You wanted it all sorted out immediately. If not yesterday. You even insisted it was me that did it, God help me. Well, here I am. But don't think you can sneer at me. I won't stand for it.'

He blinked. 'I can see that.'

Nicky narrowed her eyes suspiciously. He was not laughing—well, not openly. She checked on the security of her dressing gown anyway.

'I shall do what I came for,' she said loftily. 'And then I shall leave.'

But it didn't seem that was what he had in mind at all.

'We will need to talk about that.'

Nicky would have liked to sweep out. But she had a pheasant casserole that was beginning to smell faintly of caramel. It clearly needed attention.

So she turned her shoulder and busied herself with the dish. She ignored him loftily. But she was well aware that Esteban Tremain did not take his eyes off her. It sent a prickle of constant awareness up and down her spine. Nicky did not like it.

Sexual tension, she told herself. Nothing personal and nothing that won't go away if you don't feed it. Not surprising in the circumstances. Just don't acknowledge it and it will evaporate.

Nicky had had a lot of practice at ignoring sexual tension and she knew what she was talking about. But this was a first in her experience. She was very conscious of her nakedness under the old velvet; the damp hair that was falling out of its pins to send drips down her nape along her bare spine; his eyes on both…

She did her best to ignore him and concentrated on tasting: the pheasant needed mustard, thyme, more wine…

Esteban clearly did not like being ignored. He strolled over, standing so close that he might as well have been touching her. Nicky could feel an electric response all along her flesh. Unobtrusively, she took hold of the front of the dressing gown again, ensuring it stayed in place. It left her with only one hand to season and stir the food but it made her feel safer.

Esteban was not looking at her, however. He had picked up the wine and was inspecting the bottle critically.

'You never got this from my cellar.'

Nicky was indignant at this slur on her professional ethics.

'Of course not. I brought everything with me.'

'Impressive.' He put the bottle down. 'Who is he?'

Nicky was tasting the dark gravy.

'Who?' she said absently.

His voice was light but there was an undertone of anger when he said, 'The guy all this is for.'

Nicky froze. Then, very slowly, she put down the ladle, and turned to face him.

'I—beg—your—pardon?'

'It's quite a package. Gourmet dinner. Good wine.' His twitched his nose and gave her a sexy, slanting smile. But his eyes were not smiling. 'Scented bath,' he finished softly.

Nicky increased the grip on her dressing gown until her hand shook with tension. The look she sent him held acute dislike.

'So?'

'So—it all adds up to a lover.' There was an edge to the casual voice. 'Lucky man.'

Nicky's head went back as if he had hit her. It was all too horribly reminiscent of that scene on the *Calico Jane*. Why, *why* had she chosen this week of all times to rerun that particular bit of memory?

Esteban did not seem to notice her reaction. He was smiling. It was not a nice smile. 'Is he upstairs now? Or are you still waiting for him to get here?'

His tone was tolerant but Nicky had the fleeting impression of fierce anger. It was swept away in anger of her own, as great as any she could remember.

Shaking with it, she said dulcetly, 'Why would it matter to you?'

His eyes narrowed. Quite suddenly he stopped even pretending to be amused. 'It's my house.'

'Very territorial,' she mocked.

He took a step forward. It brought him close. Too close. Nicky found she was arching backwards over the countertop to get away from him.

'And it's my time,' he said. 'I assume I will be getting a bill for this service?'

She stayed mocking but it was an effort. 'Not at all. With the compliments of the management—'

She broke off. For a moment the mask flicked aside and Esteban Tremain looked absolutely murderous. Nicky pulled herself together. This was no way to placate a dissatisfied client. She dropped the mockery. 'There will be no bill.'

Their eyes locked. To her fury, Nicky felt herself still straining away from him. It was pure instinct.

And then the unthinkable happened. The tense arc of her body finally put too great a strain on the knotted tie at her waist. Suddenly aware, Nicky tried to grab it. Too late. The dressing gown fell open and then, before she was aware, slid off shoulders still slippery from her oiled bath.

'Oh, *no*,' she cried.

Esteban's eyes flared wide. There was an instant's disbelieving silence.

'Spectacular.' There was an odd note in his voice, as if he was not as unmoved as he wanted to be.

Nicky decided she hated him. For a paralysed moment she could not move. That steady gaze seemed almost to have stopped time. It was like a touch. Like a caress. Like a memory from ten years ago.

And then his eyes lifted and gazed straight into hers. Nicky felt the ground fall away. She made a small panicky sound. At once his eyelids dropped, masking his expression. It was as if a current had been switched off. Nicky swallowed. She felt as if she had been let off something she dreaded. With clumsy fingers, she hauled the dressing gown back up her arms and clutched it across her breasts, hard.

Fortunately the countertop had stopped it sliding all the way to the floor. So at least she did not have to humiliate herself by scrabbling at his feet to gather it up. But that was not much of a consolation. Not when Esteban's eyes lingered with blatant appreciation on the shadowed cleft between her breasts which the clutched garment still revealed.

Nicky said bitterly, 'You could at least *pretend* to be a gentleman.'

His eyes glinted. 'And what does that mean? Pass you a saucepan to hide your modesty?'

Nicky redoubled her grip on the gown. She glared. 'You could stop—staring.'

Esteban propped himself against the kitchen table and folded his arms.

'I could,' he agreed cordially. 'Give me one good reason why I should.'

'It's not kind,' she flashed.

He pretended to give it serious consideration. Then he shook his head.

'Not good enough. I've never claimed to be kind.'

'I can believe it,' Nicky muttered.

'Well, then.' He shrugged.

Nicky met his eyes with a shock. The current was on again. Her face, her whole body felt hot. Hurriedly, she levered herself away from the countertop.

'I am going to get dressed,' she announced.

His smile flickered into life again. 'Shame,' he murmured.

Nicky recognised deliberate provocation. She ignored it.

'I shall get dressed,' she repeated. 'Then I shall finish cooking the supper.'

Esteban was all politeness. 'And who gets to eat it?'

Nicky looked at him with dislike. 'You. Tonight if you like. Or I can put it in the game larder for tomorrow. The deep freeze isn't working.' Her idea suddenly returned. 'Except that—'

He interrupted. Back on form, thought Nicky sourly.

'You mean you cooked a meal and no one was supposed to eat it?' He sounded incredulous.

Nicky shrugged. Carefully.

'I'm putting the machines through their paces. What happens to the resulting meal is immaterial.'

'Isn't that rather a waste?'

'Maybe. But it's more ethical than what you had in mind,' she said with satisfaction.

His eyes narrowed. 'And what exactly do you think I had in mind?'

'I don't think,' Nicky pointed out. 'I know. You accused me of inviting a boyfriend to join me here.'

If she had hoped to discompose him, she was disappointed.

'The word I used,' he said deliberately, 'was lover.'

Nicky flushed to the roots of her hair. Embarrassment warred with indignation. Indignation won. But only just.

'I haven't forgotten,' she said grimly.

Esteban was watching her. He looked intrigued suddenly. 'And?'

'I resent the professional slur,' Nicky said with precision. 'Which is the same whether you thought I was entertaining a simple friend or the Emperor Nero.'

He let out a surprised crack of laughter. One wicked eyebrow went up.

'No lovers?' he asked outrageously.

Nicky was literally speechless.

'You're between candidates?' he pressed.

Oh, he was a barrister all right. Nicky felt as if she was on a witness stand, being grilled. She glared.

It had no effect on Esteban at all. Of course, he must be used to his victims glaring at him in impotent fury.

'Or one of the new Puritans?' he pursued ruthlessly.

'No,' Nicky choked.

'No, I thought not,' he agreed. 'It would be a terrible waste. Besides, I saw you with a man who was definitely no Puritan.'

Nicky remembered the way he had sized up Ben in the showroom. 'I wouldn't want to interrupt your social life,' he had said, sneering. But she was not explaining her brother to him, or anything else for that matter. In fact Nicky was not going to say any more to Esteban Tremain than she absolutely had to.

She said sweetly—and untruthfully—'Of course, I'm sorry to disappoint you. But before you get any more exotic ideas let me point out that this is what I always do when I'm testing a kitchen.'

Esteban clearly thought he had won that particular exchange. He smiled like a satisfied tiger.

'And you bring your own dressing gown to do it.' He looked her up and down eloquently.

Nicky gave him a glacial smile. 'I bring everything. The dressing gown in the kitchen is, I admit, a mistake.'

'Not at all. I look on it as a bonus.'

She gritted her teeth and refused to blush.

'Thank you. How flattering,' said Nicky, not meaning a word of it.

'I never flatter.'

He moved towards her. Nicky stood her ground, her eyes warning him.

She said curtly, 'I had a thought in the bath. So I came down to check the fuses in the plugs on the machines. But as you're so smart you'll already have done that before complaining, right?'

'So you're an electrician as well.'

Esteban looked at her with admiration. Nicky was quite certain it was mocking. She wanted to scream. She wanted to hit him. She wanted to dance with temper. 'Fine,' she said, finally losing it. 'You find the screwdriver. You do it.'

She stalked past him without another look.

The bath water was cold, of course. She pulled on her grubby clothes rapidly, muttering to herself. How on earth could she have been so stupid as to let Esteban Tremain see how he was getting to her?

It had to be because she had let herself think about what happened all those years ago. She could not imagine why she had done so. It must have been seeing Ben that had brought it all back. It was nonsense to think it could have anything to do with Esteban Tremain, no matter how autocratic his manner. It was not his autocratic manner that she remembered about Steve.

In spite of the central heating, the room was getting chilly as the dark closed in. Nicky went back to her bedroom and rummaged in her overnight case for a loose wool jacket. She dragged it on and turned back to the chest of drawers, seeking her image in the spotted mirror that stood on top of it.

She was fluffing out her drying hair absently when her eye fell on the photographs. There were several: a studio portrait

of a beautiful woman with wistful eyes in an oval silver
frame; a tall military-looking man in formal clothes at a wed-
ding; a posed group of men, clearly a team of some kind;
several informal pictures of people, dogs, children, boats…

Boats. And one particular picture.

Nicky stopped fluffing her hair and picked it up. She could
hardly believe her eyes.

It looked like a holiday snap. It showed three people on
the deck of a catamaran. They were holding up champagne
flutes in a toast and laughing. One was a spectacularly beautiful woman. The two men were in shorts, shirtless, their
bodies gleaming with health. All three were wearing sunglasses as they looked into the camera.

Nicky looked at the taller man and felt a flicker of panic.
I don't believe this, she thought. And then, But of course I
do. Only I'm not ready for it.

Slowly, reluctantly, she turned the leather picture frame
over. It was there on the back, in neat script. '*Glen Tandy
III*, Gibraltar. Francesca Moran. Fernando Arauho. Esteban
Tremain.'

She turned it back. She had thought she would never forget
that face.

Well, her conscious mind had not recognised him without
those alienating tinted glasses. But something had. Something visceral had been plucking at her ever since she'd heard
his voice on the phone. Why else were all these hateful memories stalking her? Usually she suppressed them without difficulty.

Nicky looked again at the photograph in her hand.

The taller man, laughing on the deck of his boat, was
Esteban Tremain. That was what it said on the back of the
snap. And anyway she could see it, in the set of the shoulders
and the arrogant tilt of the head.

But he was also a man called Steve. And he had ruined
her life.

CHAPTER FIVE

NICKY sat down hard on the side of the four-poster bed. She felt cold with shock. For ten years the man had haunted her. And when she saw him again she did not even *recognise* him? She could not believe it.

But then she thought about it.

That was not true, was it? Or not the whole truth. She had recognised him all right. At some deep, unconscious level she had *known*. From the first day, when he had looked at her across the showroom, a part of her had known. Even in the distance that dark figure had set a chord of memory thrumming.

Why else had she kept so far away from the Hallam Hall contract? Oh, of course you could say it was chance, that she was doing other things for other clients. But the truth was that she had not even asked a question or glanced at a plan until he'd rung. Then, and only then, she had picked up the file. Was there a single other Springdown client about whom she knew so little? Had taken care to know so little about, Nicky admitted now.

'Oh, God.' The strangled sound was wrenched out of her.

How could it have happened? You would have thought it was impossible. A crazy coincidence across the distance of ten years and a quarter of the world. Nicky did not believe in coincidence.

Just for a moment, her heart lifted. Maybe it was not true after all. She had been remembering too much in the last few days. Maybe she was just applying it to an innocent stranger. Maybe she was mistaken. Maybe…

She turned back to the picture.

She was not mistaken. She wished with all her heart that she was. But he was Steve, all right.

There was no escaping it. Those blanked eyes were the last piece in the jigsaw puzzle. Now she saw clearly what her senses, more alert than her mind, had been picking up all along.

God help me, I even knew his smell, Nicky thought.

She passed a shaking hand over her face. What was she going to do? Go downstairs and talk to him as if nothing had changed?

No, she thought. She could not do it. She still remembered that scene on the boat in every wince-making detail, and she could recall every word he had ever said to her.

As for that harsh kiss on the beach—well, if she was honest, had it not spoiled her for every kiss since? Andrew Bolton was only the latest in a long, long line of men who did not know what they had said or done to turn Nicky to ice. And the worst of it was that it was not their fault.

Every time a man took her in his arms, she had to fight to remind herself that he was not Steve and he did not despise her. When they touched her in passion all she could think of was another night and the stars and an angry man walking away from her. And she froze.

Nicky drew an unsteady breath. She put the photo frame down very carefully. It seemed important to restore it to the exact spot. She felt very cold and slightly light-headed.

She remembered a little too clearly the men she had dated in the last ten years. It was not a comfortable memory. Oh, she had not told them she froze when they touched her. Of course she had not. She was a modern woman. She knew how to smile and flirt and kiss. She just did it all with a little metronome ticking in her head, marking the seconds until the man lost interest. And, when he did, she made sure she was the first to walk away.

Nicky looked at the photograph and thought, I have never kissed a man without thinking of him.

She shut her eyes.

'I can't bear it,' she said aloud.

Unexpectedly, the sound of her own voice steadied her. She opened her eyes. What on earth was she going to do?

Her instinct was to run. As far and as fast as her little car would take her. But she only had to think about that for a second to realise she could not. Or not without getting into a whole maze of explanations she could bear even less: to Caroline and the other assistants at Springdown, to Martin de Vries and, not least, to Esteban Tremain himself.

At the thought, Nicky shuddered convulsively. So far the only good thing about the whole mess was that Esteban Tremain did not have the slightest idea who she was. He had probably forgotten the whole incident as soon as it happened, of course. After all, a teenage beach bunny wasn't going to have much impact on a man as sophisticated as he was, even ten years ago. In the interim he had metamorphosed from Steve to Esteban and acquired a worldliness that hit you between the eyes. So he certainly would not remember her now.

She found she was pressing her hands together so hard that her wrists shook. In the mirror it looked as if she was praying. Nicky gave a shaky laugh and loosened her grip.

Of course he would not remember her now. Thank God. And it was up to her to make sure that it stayed that way. She could go down and act as if nothing had happened. She *could*.

She would be as sweet as pie to him. She would busy herself so totally with his damned kitchen that he would think of her as just another piece of equipment. Until she could get away, she would be so neutral, she would just disappear into the background. No confrontations, no arguments. She would agree with his every suggestion. She would challenge nothing.

It should not be too difficult. A man like Esteban Tremain was not going to take too much notice of a humble kitchen advisor, was he? She tried hard not to remember that he had already taken notice of her to the tune of three first-class rows and a toe-curling appreciation of her exposed flesh.

Taking her courage in both hands, Nicky went downstairs. Esteban was still in the kitchen. He had discarded his jacket for a dark sweater. He must have rumpled his hair as he'd pulled it on. To Nicky's dismay, his slight air of dishevelment made him look a lot more like the man she remembered on the beach. She swallowed hard.

I must not think of him as Steve, she thought. *I must not.*

He had found a bottle of champagne and two glasses. He must have just opened it. The bottle stood on the kitchen table with a faint plume of smoke escaping from its neck.

'What's this?' said Nicky, distracted.

He looked up from the task and gave her an unexpectedly charming smile. Nicky blinked.

Careful, she thought.

'Peace offering,' he said lightly.

He poured, tilting the glasses professionally so the pale liquid did not foam over the top. He put the bottle down and surveyed the pale gold flutes with satisfaction before he strolled over. He held out a glass to her.

Nicky did not take it.

'Where did you get that?' she demanded. She was suspicious of the charm and shaken by her own reaction to it. 'I didn't bring any champagne. And there was nothing in the fridge.'

'We have a cellar.'

He took her hand and curled her fingers round the cold glass. Nicky shuddered. *How* she remembered that touch.

Esteban gave her an enigmatic look.

'Yes, I agree,' he said provocatively.

Nicky nearly dropped her glass. Was he reading her mind? *'What?'*

His eyes laughed at her. 'The champagne,' he explained. 'Just cold enough.'

But he ran one long finger lightly across her knuckles where her hand was closed convulsively round the stem of the wine glass. The touch left Nicky breathless—and in no doubt that he was reading her like a book. *Help,* she thought.

Esteban turned back to the table and retrieved his own glass. He raised it to her.

'Your very good health,' he said softly.

In spite of all her resolutions, Nicky did not find she could toast him back.

'Why champagne?'

She knew she sounded sulky and could not help it. His dark brows twitched together as if she had hit a nerve suddenly.

'That voice,' he said.

Nicky was wary. 'What?'

'You have a memorable voice. The trouble is, I can't remember where I've heard it.'

Panic flared in Nicky, as sudden and violent as a forest fire. She fought it down. But not quickly enough.

'What did I say?' he demanded.

Oh, yes, he was certainly reading her like the simplest book in his library.

'N-nothing.'

He scanned her face. 'Have we met before?'

This was terrible. Nicky knit her brows, pretending to think.

'I don't remember any Esteban Tremain.' It helped that it was the literal truth.

She could see he was not convinced. Alarm fluttered in her throat. She curbed it. Smile, goddammit. *Smile,* she told herself.

It was clearly not very successful.

'Don't look like that,' he said. 'I'm not going to jump on you.'

Nicky bristled at the superior tone. The obvious retort leapt to her lips: 'That makes a change'. Just in time she stopped herself, folding her lips together tightly. It was a close-run thing, though.

And not before Esteban had seen her reaction. His smile died and his eyes grew keen.

'*Now* what have I said?'

Nicky shook her head, taking a sip of champagne. Esteban sent her a shrewd look.

'You're as jumpy as a flea on a hot plate. Is that my fault? I know we got off on the wrong foot—' he began. Nicky could not help herself. She gave a snort of laughter. How right he was and how little he knew it.

Esteban was disconcerted. 'I'm sorry?'

'I didn't say anything,' Nicky assured him hurriedly. The shock of discovery was beginning to wear off. She gave him a sweet smile. 'You were talking about the wrong foot?'

He looked at her narrowly for a moment. Then gave a slight shrug.

'The first time we spoke. I was already in a temper,' he admitted.

It was the last thing Nicky had expected.

'You mean when you shouted down the phone at me?'

Esteban had the grace to look uncomfortable.

'I was furious about something else entirely. When I couldn't get hold of de Vries it was just the last straw.'

'So you took it out on me,' she agreed pleasantly.

Esteban stopped being apologetic. He looked irritated. 'It was a perfectly legitimate complaint.'

'You were very nasty.'

He made an impatient noise. 'Well, now I'm trying to make amends.' He raised his glass to her.

Nicky did not drink in response. 'Try harder.'

'That's not going to be easy if you won't meet me half-way,' he pointed out. 'Come on, drink your champagne and let's start again.'

For a moment she was speechless. He'd ruined her life and he wanted her to wave it aside and *start again*?

But of course he did not know he had ruined her life. Unless she decided to tell him, that was. And Nicky thought that she would rather die.

'To our better acquaintance,' he was saying.

Nicky blenched.

'To our better understanding,' she temporised.

He was too quick to miss the way she had changed his toast. His brows rose.

'Nicola Piper, you're an unforgiving woman,' he said softly. 'I can see I shall have to do something about that.'

She managed not to wince. 'I wouldn't advise it.' It was light enough but there was no disguising the fact that she meant it.

Esteban looked at her speculatively. 'You don't think I can change your mind?'

She shook her head. 'I'm a pretty hopeless case on the unforgiving front.'

'But don't you know that's my profession?' he said softly. 'I specialise in reversing hopeless cases.'

She said more sharply than she intended, 'I don't know anything about you at all.'

And don't want to, said her tone. To her annoyance, Esteban Tremain laughed as if he had won his first point. His eyes danced. His charm was as heady as wine—and he knew it. Careful, Nicky said to herself.

'What an excellent place to start.' He stood up and made her a bow. 'Let me introduce—Esteban Felipe Tremain, age thirty-eight, marital status unattached, qualifications numerous, hobbies sailing and baiting harmless kitchen planners.'

He held out his hand. His dark eyes were so warm, you could almost believe that the charm was for real, she thought. Careful, Nicky.

'Pleased to meet you—what do I call you? Nicola? Nick?'

'Nicky,' she agreed reluctantly. She could not think of any way to deny him her name but it felt like another small surrender to that lethal charm.

Even more reluctantly, she took his hand.

'Truce,' she offered, trying not to remember the last time they had touched.

He pursed his mouth. 'Oh, I think I want a lot more than a truce.'

Nicky was sure she was being baited again. There was only one way to deal with that. Fight fire with fire.

'You're getting a lot more,' she told him dulcetly.

His eyebrows rose. She retrieved her hand with some difficulty.

'You're getting dinner,' she concluded.

He gave a choke of surprised laughter. 'Good point.' Nicky felt a small glow of triumph. She put her champagne glass down and removed herself from that disturbing closeness. She had the ideal excuse, busying herself with the food.

Over her shoulder she said, 'When would you like to eat?'

Esteban laughed lazily. 'What luxury. I usually microwave a pizza.'

Nicky looked wryly at the dead microwave. 'Not here, you don't.'

As soon as she said it, she could have kicked herself. What a chance for him to start complaining about Springdown again! But he did not.

Instead he picked up the bottle and replenished her glass.

'I was talking about my own place in London. My stepfather hates fast food. When we planned the kitchen, we slipped in the microwave when he wasn't looking.'

Nicky was intrigued in spite of herself. 'Your stepfather? But I thought this was your house.'

He shrugged. 'Technically it is. He made it over to me some years ago. But it's his home; he was born here. I only get down here every couple of months. He lives here.'

Nicky looked eloquently round the characterless kitchen.

'Not so as you'd notice.'

Briefly his expression was sombre. 'He's been away.'

Absently he topped up his own glass. Nicky thought he would take the wine to his room and unpack but he did not. Instead he settled himself at the kitchen table as if he belonged there. As, she supposed with a slight shock, he did.

He looked round approvingly.

'The kitchen looks better.'

'You mean with some food in it?' Nicky said tartly.

He nodded slowly. 'I suppose I do. And light and some

good smells as well, of course. It's been a long time.' He looked bleak suddenly.

Nicky felt an unwelcome twinge of sympathy. Where was the 'very good friend' the article talked about? If she was the woman Esteban had mentioned trying out the appliances, why hadn't she made the kitchen her own?

She said with constraint, 'I am sorry, Mr Tremain. I didn't mean to pry.'

He came back to the present with a grimace. 'You weren't prying and my name is Esteban.'

Nicky did not say anything. She did not need to. Her silence said for her how totally she rejected the idea of calling this man by his Christian name.

Esteban considered her thoughtfully.

'You really don't like me, do you?'

Nicky shifted uncomfortably. 'Are you surprised?' she hedged.

It was not the answer he wanted. 'Well, that's honest, I suppose.' He surveyed her for an unsmiling moment. Then he said abruptly, 'Why do I make you nervous?'

Nicky's heart lurched sickeningly. The last time he had looked at her like that was on a boat in the Caribbean and—

'You don't!' she said loudly.

Esteban's eyes narrowed in an arrested expression. 'Oh, that voice,' he muttered. '*Where* have we met before?'

To her consternation, he leaned forward across the table and took her by the wrist.

The floor surged under Nicky's feet like the deck of a boat. *Stop it,* her mind yelled, panic-stricken. She wrenched herself away.

'Don't *touch* me.'

This time she had really startled him. For a moment she read blank amazement in the dark eyes. And not just amazement, either. Attraction, sizzling and irrefutable. When he looked at her like that, Nicky shot back over the years in the

blink of an eyelid. She was a trembling teenager again, surrendering to a magnetic pull she did not understand.

Not again, thought Nicky, her mouth suddenly dry. *Never
again.*

She fought for control. 'I'm here to sort out your kitchen,'
she said crisply. 'Not play games with you.'

'Who's playing?'

Her every instinct was to retreat. By a supreme effort of
will she managed not to. Instead she took a step towards him
and slapped her hand down on the table between them. It
made the glass and bottle ring.

'Stop right there,' she said with quiet force. 'You know
perfectly well you've been baiting me since the moment you
arrived.'

And before in London, she thought, though she was not
going to say it. She heard again, 'You're the blonde.'

'You push me around.' She was almost shouting. 'You
won't tell me anything—not about who uses the kitchen, not
about anything. You— Oh what's the use?'

There was silence. Nicky was sure he could hear her heart
thundering. She put a hand to her throat to quieten the pulse
that drummed there.

Esteban watched the gesture through narrowed eyes.

'I think this is about more than inadequate briefing,' he
said at last.

'No,' said Nicky, her voice shaking.

It was exactly the same unheeded protest she had made on
the beach all those years ago. Even Nicky could hear the tell-
tale tremor. She shut her eyes. How long before Esteban realised that the last time he'd heard her voice she had been
shouting 'I hate you'? How long before she said it again?

He said conversationally, 'Are you always this dramatic?'

Nicky opened her eyes. He was looking annoyed. But not
angry; not embarrassed and guilty; not like a man who'd
realised a disreputable incident from his past had risen to
haunt him.

She took her hand from her throat. Disaster averted. This time anyway.

'I don't like being messed about,' she said with truth.

'Evidently.'

He seemed to take a decision. He gave a quick shrug.

'OK, you can have the full run-down. It's no big deal. My stepfather was getting too old to run the estate but he wanted to keep it in the family. Since my mother died, I'm all the family he's got. I took over the administrative side of things and he carried on living here. I took control of the land. He ran the house. At least that was the theory—'

He broke off, lapsing into a brown study. Nicky thought of the smell as she'd unlocked the front door. It had not smelled like a house that was lived in. She said so.

'What?' He looked up. 'Oh. Shrewd of you. No, it isn't. It's been empty for the best part of a year. Except when I can get down here. Which isn't as often as I should.'

'So why the kitchen?'

He was puzzled. 'What?'

'Nobody lives here full time,' she pointed out. 'You're happy with microwaved pizza. Why the glossy-mag kitchen?'

'Oh, that.' He sounded bored. 'My stepfather has always wanted to come back. He's been ill, you see. The doctors said it would probably be good for him to come home but he couldn't live on his own. The district nurse would visit but he needed a full-time housekeeper if he was going to live here again. The person I—' he hesitated '—had in mind said the existing kitchen was a death trap. So my stepfather stayed in his nursing home and the builders came in to the Hall.'

'And then even the new kitchen didn't work,' Nicky said. She felt an unwelcome compunction. She did not like it. She did not want to start feeling sympathetic towards Esteban Tremain.

'And the potential housekeeper walked out. With a few choice words about false pretences.'

Nicky began to see why he had lost his temper with Springdown.

'Have you found a replacement?'

'I haven't even looked yet.' Esteban sounded weary suddenly. 'I thought it was sorted. Now I'll have to see my stepfather before I go to New Zealand.'

'You're going away?'

Esteban looked up and all weariness fell away.

'Just for a job. I'll be back in two weeks.'

He gave her the sudden, wicked smile she was beginning to recognise. It made her stomach turn over. She was beginning to recognise that too.

'Why, Nicky! You sound almost as if you'd miss me,' he said softly.

Nicky stiffened. He laughed.

Careful, she thought.

'You're so easy to tease,' he said with satisfaction. 'Very rewarding.'

At least he wasn't asking questions she didn't want to answer, Nicky told herself. That was what she wanted, wasn't it? But his easy superiority set her teeth on edge.

He stood up and stretched.

'Since the water and the heating are on and supper is in the oven, I think I'm going to indulge myself. Pretend I'm Mr Average come home from a hard day at the office.'

Nicky tensed. She knew he was teasing again but she could not help herself.

She said acidly, 'Don't get carried away.'

Esteban grinned. 'Don't worry. I only meant I'll unpack my briefcase. Make a few phone calls. Take a shower.' His eyes gleamed. 'Come down and finish the rest of the champagne with you.'

Nicky stayed cool. 'I look forward to it,' she said untruthfully. She did not like the sound of it at all. She just hoped she could handle it.

'So do I.' He gave her a long, speculative look. 'We have so much to talk about.'

She liked the sound of that even less.

'H-have we?'

'Two life histories. To say nothing of kitchen appliances,' he said blandly.

And, with an enigmatic smile, he strolled out of the kitchen.

CHAPTER SIX

DINNER turned out to be less than the ordeal of intimacy which Nicky feared. Esteban was preoccupied. Oh, he was polite, even complimentary about the food, but she had the feeling that he was far away, turning over a problem in his mind that he was not willing to share with anyone.

So it must have been sheer perversity that prompted her to say, 'Problems?'

He shrugged. 'Nothing new.'

The meal was over. Esteban was sitting at the kitchen table, idly shaving slivers off the Cheddar cheese she had brought, frowning. At her question, he'd looked up abruptly as if he had forgotten anyone else was there.

His eyes met hers. Nicky almost jumped at the impact. It shocked her. She could keep telling herself the attraction was all in the past but the moment she looked into those dark, dark eyes it was *there*.

Esteban was beginning to sense it too, she could tell. Now his eyes narrowed on her hair as if the golden strands could tell him something. Nicky put up a defensive hand and found she had lost the clip which kept it in a neat queue at the back of her neck. Hurriedly she bundled it into a knot and rummaged in her pocket for an elastic band.

'Don't do that.' Esteban seemed as if he could not keep his eyes off her hair. He leaned forward and prised it gently out of its loose knot. 'Leave it free.'

She caught it and held it into the back of her neck.

'I prefer—' Her voice scraped. She cleared her throat and started again. 'I prefer to keep it tied back. It's more professional.'

'But work is finished for the day.'

But keeping a professional distance wasn't, Nicky thought grimly. Though she was not going to say that to Esteban Tremain. Going by his behaviour this evening, he would only take it as a challenge.

'There's still the washing-up. And that machine wasn't working either.' She stood up and started to gather plates. 'Unless you did check the fuses?'

He made an impatient gesture. 'I'm willing to buy one duff fuse. Not—' he looked round the kitchen, counting '—a dozen or more.'

'I thought the same myself,' Nicky admitted. 'Still, there's an outside chance, I suppose. Maybe the installers had a bad batch of fuses. I ought to check before I call in the mechanics.'

Esteban shrugged, supremely uninterested.

'If you want. But I warn you, I'm going to light the fire in the study. When it's lit I want you to stop working and come and have coffee with me.'

Nicky did not like the sound of that. She did not want to spend the rest of the evening in front of a blazing fire with Esteban Tremain. There was something horribly intimate about open fires.

So she made a noncommittal noise and finished clearing the table.

'As long as that's understood,' he said. It was soft but quite, quite determined.

Nicky gave a little inward shiver and did not look at him.

'Understood.'

He went.

Nicky switched off the current to the kitchen power points. Then she collected her all-purpose screwdriver from her bag and dived under the countertop to remove the plug from the electric socket.

Five minutes later she was sitting cross-legged in the middle of the kitchen floor, surrounded by three dismembered plugs. She looked at them in disbelief. The screwdriver fell from her hand with a clatter. She did not notice.

'This is *crazy*,' she said aloud.

Esteban came back into the kitchen, dusting off his hands. 'A fine healthy blaze—' he began.

And stopped at the sight of Nicky sitting on the floor. One look at her frozen face and he crossed to her in quick concern.

'What is it?'

Mutely she held out a plug to him. He took a cursory glance and shrugged, puzzled.

'So?'

Nicky realised that she was very scared. It was such a *malicious* thing for someone to do. Unbalanced.

She swallowed. 'The fuse wasn't faulty. The wire had been mutilated. And there wasn't a fuse in the plug at all. Or this.' She picked up the flex to the kettle with its stripped plug. 'Or this.' A state-of-the-art steam iron. 'I'll bet all these machines are the same. That's why the gas on the stove worked but the electric controls didn't.'

He turned the plug over in his hand. 'Odd.' He picked up the mangled flex and frowned. 'I think Springdown needs to take a serious look at its quality control. Still, easy enough to put right now you've found the hitch.'

Nicky felt very cold.

'You don't understand,' she said. 'It's not a hitch. It's deliberate.'

'*What?*' He stared at her.

She shook her head, still not quite believing it herself. Not *wanting* to believe it.

'I didn't check the fuses because, like you, I thought they couldn't *all* have gone. And anyway Springdown give the installers worksheets. The last thing they do is fuse the plug, connect the machine and check the wiring is OK. It's a whole section on the form.' She waved a hand at her file, now on the cherry-wood dresser. 'Every single one of the forms has been filled out showing the electric plug in working order.'

He was unimpressed. 'Workmen have been known to falsify worksheets. And if it's the last job they'd have been in a hurry.'

'Different workmen,' said Nicky. 'Different days. Different suppliers.' She gestured round the kitchen. 'There isn't a fuse in any machine I've looked at. Someone must have taken them out.'

Esteban stared. 'Taken them out? That's stupid.'

Nicky shivered. 'It's such an easy way to disable a machine. When I was working in advertising, we used to do it all the time when we had children on photo shoots.'

Esteban said categorically, 'No one would have done such a stupid thing deliberately.'

She touched the damaged flex. 'That sort of damage can't happen by chance. It has to be vandalism.'

'But what's the point?'

Nicky looked at the half plug in her hand. 'That's what makes it so nasty. Pointless and mean.'

Esteban took the plug out of her hand and put it on the countertop.

'Don't you understand?' Her voice rose. 'Someone set out to disable your kitchen.'

His reaction was not what she expected. He did not rage or scoff. Instead he hunkered down in front of her and turned her chin gently towards him.

'It has really upset you,' he said on a note of discovery.

Nicky shook her head. But there was not much point in denying it when the truth was written all over her face.

Esteban stroked her cheek with an oddly comforting finger.

'This is no big deal, Nicky. Probably just a mistake by some half-trained assistant who isn't very bright.'

'You don't have to be bright to know that a plug needs a fuse,' she flashed.

He tucked a swathe of golden hair behind her ear absently.

'Even if you're right and it was deliberate, so what? It's scarcely life-threatening. Just a prank.'

It did not feel like a prank to Nicky. 'It's so—spiteful. And underhand.'

Esteban was unmoved by the thought. He swung down on to the floor beside her and put an arm round her shoulders.

'Sure. But it's only a temporary inconvenience. I contacted Springdown. Springdown got you down here. You'll put fuses in the plugs. End of problem.'

'Except that whoever did this is still out there.'

His arm fell from her shoulders. His voice cooled noticeably. 'There's no need for melodrama.'

Nicky turned her head. His eyes were very close. They were expressionless. Don't ask any more, they said.

She said involuntarily, 'Have you got any enemies?'

He looked at her with an unnerving lack of expression for a minute. Then he smiled, a crooked slant of the sensual mouth that got nowhere near his eyes.

'Sure. Who hasn't?'

'Enemies who would want to hurt you?'

'I've got a better class of enemies than people who would waste their time messing about with dishwashers.'

Nicky remembered rather suddenly that he was superior, dictatorial and altogether hateful. She pushed away from him and stood up.

'I think I've just been put in my place,' she remarked.

She turned away.

Esteban came lightly to his feet.

'Nicky?'

He turned her back to face him. His touch was quite gentle but somehow it brooked no resistance. Something inside Nicky went very still. He searched her face.

'What is it about you?' he said, almost to himself.

Her mind whirled. But she stood unmoving under his hands. Like a trapped animal whose only chance of escape is playing dead, she thought.

Esteban shook his head as if to clear it.

'Put it this way.' He sounded strained. 'Most of the people who wish me ill are international criminals I have failed to keep out of jail. Bomb under the car, maybe. Fuse out of the dishwasher—no way.'

His hands were warm. Even under the old sweater she could feel the heat of his fingers against her shoulders. She felt as if she was drowning in warm, silky water. Nicky struggled to concentrate.

'Bomb under the car?'

Was it his pulse or hers she could hear? It slammed through her, slow and sweet and almost deafening.

Esteban's eyes were uncomfortably acute.

'Joke.'

Nicky swallowed and the thunder of the pulse subsided. She removed herself carefully from his grip.

'A very bad one.' It was clipped because her every instinct was to gasp for air and she did not want him to see it.

He shrugged. 'Just putting the thing in context. No one's going to sabotage a kitchen, for heaven's sake.'

'It depends what you think is important,' Nicky pointed out. Her breathing, thank God, was coming back under control. 'Annoyed any good cooks lately?'

'No, of course not. I—' He broke off abruptly.

Nicky took the other half of the plug away from him and turned away. It was better when she was not looking at him. Then the terrible vulnerabilities of her teenage self retreated into the past where they belonged.

The modern, professional Nicky said briskly, 'I've only got a couple of fuses in my bag. I'll wire up the dishwasher tonight so we can use it. I'll get some more fuses and do the rest in the morning. Then you'll have a fully functioning kitchen and I can go back to London and get on with my life.'

He was frowning. 'What?'

She repeated it, patiently. Esteban did not seem very interested.

'Oh, yes. Of course,' he said absently. 'Look—why don't you make us some coffee? I've got a couple of calls to make.'

He walked out without another word.

Nicky breathed more easily. But she found that her hands were shaking as she made the coffee. Was that her fear of possible saboteurs? Or of Esteban? Or—it was not a welcome thought—of herself?

It took her time to find the library. In the end it was only the sound of his voice which led her to it, down a flagged passage where the tapestries wafted in the old house's draughts. She was shivering by the time she pushed open the door. Not entirely from the cold.

As he had promised, the fire was blazing. A huge log lay across a vast fire basket, glowing red-hot, while flames danced up through logs and fir cones around it. It drew Nicky like a magnet.

The heavy velvet curtains were still open. In the blackness beyond the long windows, Nicky thought she could make out the shifting shadow of the sea. That was where Esteban was standing, one foot on a window seat, his back to the room. He was talking rapidly into a telephone. He did not hear her come in.

'—completely stupid,' he was saying icily.

Nicky stopped dead. She had heard that tone before. When he'd taken her to pieces in the showroom. On a beach when he'd said, 'That was what you really wanted, wasn't it?' She shivered. She felt sorry for whoever was on the receiving end this time.

Esteban did not notice her. She had the impression he was very angry.

'I did not ask you to do me any favours,' he said in a level voice. 'It was a job, pure and simple. If you didn't want it, all you had to do was say so. Not play childish tricks.'

The other person clearly burst into speech. Esteban waited.

'I don't believe you,' he said finally.

He cut the connection and slammed his mobile phone shut.

'You're a real charmer on the phone, aren't you?' Nicky remarked drily.

He swung round, startled.

She raised her eyebrows. 'I gather you've thought of some-one who might have sabotaged your kitchen after all.'

She looked round for somewhere to put down the mugs of

coffee that was not an antique. There was nowhere. She compromised by putting them on the edge of the hearth.

She held out her hands to the blaze.

He came over to the pool of light and warmth in front of the fire.

'It's nothing to worry about. Just someone being silly.'

Was he trying to reassure her? It hadn't sounded silly. She shivered.

'Was it a disgruntled cook?'

He kicked a log into blazing life.

'In a way.'

'Still not a very high-class enemy?'

He looked at her broodingly for a moment.

'Let's say I haven't been very clever about my dealings with that particular person.'

'Really?' There was an edge to Nicky's voice. 'Not very clever? Or not very kind?'

Esteban winced. He sank down on to an ancient sofa at right angles to the fire.

'Probably both,' he admitted after a pause. He leaned forward, changing the subject decisively. 'You found the coffee, then?'

Nicky took the hint and passed the mug up to him.

'I brought it with me. Like everything else. Including the kettle.'

'How efficient.' He took the mug. 'Thank you. Is that normal or just because you were coming out to the wilds of rural Cornwall?'

'Standard procedure,' Nicky assured him.

It was a relief to talk about something that did not stir up her unmanageable memory. For the first time she could hear herself sounding almost friendly.

'You daren't use anything in a client's kitchen. It might be the very special vintage mustard they searched half of France for. Then you can go and put a couple of tablespoons of it in the stew. End of good relationship.'

He pushed away the tiredness to allow himself to be entertained. 'It sounds terrifying. Do you enjoy it?'

Nicky sipped her own coffee. 'It's only a small part of my job. Not the best bit, I admit.'

He cocked an eyebrow. 'Don't like cooking?'

'Cooking's fine. I don't like—' Too late, she stopped.

Esteban laughed softly. 'Don't like dealing with clients, eh?'

'It is not,' Nicky admitted, 'my strongest point.'

'Why not?'

'I—er—don't seem to have the rapport,' Nicky said carefully.

'You surprise me. They can't all be as unreasonable as I am,' he murmured provocatively.

Nicky was not rising to that one. 'Most of our clients are women who are going to spend more time in their kitchens than I have ever done in my life. Martin understands them. His wife is a chef. Their family life is centred on the kitchen. So he can imagine what the client needs. I can't, really.'

Esteban leaned forward. 'So where is your family life centred?'

'I live alone,' she said unexpansively.

His eyes flickered, registering the information. But he was much too subtle to pursue it.

'OK. So where was your family life centred when you were a child?'

Nicky hesitated. Then realised it would not betray her if she told him the truth.

'On a boat,' she said briefly.

Hundreds of children lived on boats, after all.

'Ah,' he said, as if he had been given the answer to a question he had not asked.

Nicky's eyes flew to his face in alarm. He saw it. His eyebrows went up.

'So that's how you know Martin de Vries,' he explained slowly. 'What did you think I meant?'

She did not answer.

He went on idly, 'In fact I met him through a yacht club myself. Maybe that's where we've met before.'

'*No!*' It was a strangled sound, frankly appalled.

'Why are you so jumpy?' Esteban leaned forward and took her chin in his hand, turning it towards him to scan her face in the firelight. 'Are you hiding a guilty secret?' It was lightly said but his face was serious.

Nicky jumped to her feet.

She said at random, 'I didn't know you and Martin were old friends.'

He did not move. But Nicky could feel him watching her measuringly.

Then he said slowly, 'We're not. My stepfather chose him to do the kitchen. De Vries built a catamaran for him years ago. Frankly it was a relief that Dad was taking an interest in anything. I just accepted it.'

So for the time being he was willing to let her off the hook. She had a nasty suspicion it would not last.

She said rapidly to deflect him, 'I'm confused. Is it you or your stepfather who makes the decisions here?'

He hesitated. Then shrugged.

'Oh, what the hell? It's no secret. Not round here anyway. If you go buying fuses in the village, you'll find out soon enough. The decisions are mine.'

Somehow Nicky was not surprised.

'My stepfather is a wonderful man but he never quite caught up with modern economics.' He sounded rueful. 'In his day, money just flowed in without him having to do any vulgar calculations. These days I do the sums. And I pay the bills.'

'That must be difficult for him,' said Nicky with instinctive sympathy.

Esteban looked surprised. 'Yes. Yes, it is. Though I would have thought— No, never mind.'

'Thought what?' Nicky demanded, bristling, though she did not quite know at what.

'Well, you don't look as if you've ever had to count the pennies yourself.'

'Then my looks belie me,' Nicky said sharply. 'I've counted the pennies. And worse.'

Esteban was taken aback. 'Worse?'

'My father was hopeless with money too.' Nicky was remembering too clearly. Unconsciously, her hands balled into fists. 'We used to take tourists out scuba diving. Some of the kind ones used to leave exaggerated tips. We were so poor, people on other boats used to give us their casts-offs—sails, equipment, even clothes sometimes. My father used to swear and my mother used to cry but the truth was we couldn't get by without them. I can understand your stepfather, believe me.'

Esteban studied her. In the leaping firelight his eyes were deeply shadowed

'Yes,' he said at last. 'Yes, I can see that you would.'

Damn, thought Nicky. Why did I tell him that? But it was too late. The only thing she could do now was rush on before he could question her.

'Having to be grateful all the time destroys you.'

Esteban glared at that, distracted as she had somehow known he would be.

'My stepfather does not have to be grateful,' he snapped.

'I bet that's not how he sees it.'

'My father rescued my mother from an impossible marriage and took me with her,' Esteban said flatly. 'Any gratitude goes in the other direction.'

Then, quite suddenly, his anger evaporated. He laughed as if it was torn out of him.

'I see why you don't like dealing with clients. Do you always jump up and down on their sorest spots?'

So she had successfully steered him away from the danger zone again. Feeling reprieved, Nicky came back to the fire and sank on to the edge of a leather chair.

'The others say that I either tell the paying customers to make up their minds or yell at them to get out of my way.'

Suddenly she was full of mischief. 'But you're my first invasion of privacy, I promise.'

Esteban's expression stilled. 'You should do that more often.'

'What, dig into clients' private lives?'

'Smile.' He leaned forward and touched one corner of her mouth. 'It looks good on you. Like a girl coming out to play after too long.'

Nicky felt as if the floor had given way under her. From relief she went to black panic. She thought, He knows.

Then, No, he doesn't know; of course he doesn't. It doesn't matter to him who I am or where I come from, he thinks he can do whatever he likes with me—just as he did ten years ago. This is a game to him, just as I said it was. He has not changed a bit. She shut her eyes.

He said softly, 'You must know you're a very sexy woman. A hundred times more so when you smile.'

Nicky tensed until her jaw ached. She knew this scene. She had played it so often, most recently with Andrew Bolton. They spoke in that soft, intimate tone, they teased, they touched... They *looked*. A familiar slow dread began to build.

She said harshly, 'I suppose you think that's a compliment.'

There was a small silence. Then Esteban said slowly, 'Well, I didn't think it was something to be ashamed of.'

Nicky's eyes flew open.

Frowning, he said, 'What's wrong?'

She shook her head, unable to answer.

Still in that tone of quiet reason, he said, 'All I did was say you are attractive. What's wrong with that?'

Nicky felt like a wild animal being lured out of hiding by soft words she could not trust. Oh, no, she could not afford to trust Esteban Tremain, of all men.

She swallowed. 'What makes you think I want to be attractive?' she said past the constriction in her throat.

He stroked one finger along the line of her tense jaw. The

movement was very gentle, very slow. It was hardly a touch at all. And totally intimate. Nicky thought, *Not again.*

'Don't you?' he murmured.

'No,' she said, so fiercely she felt tears well up in her eyes. She wanted to push his hand away. But she did not trust herself to touch him. Instead she jerked her head back.

The stroking finger paused, then moved again, rhythmically, hypnotically. She had to do something to break the spell. She *had* to.

'What a waste.' He sounded as if he had less than half his mind on what he was saying.

She looked him squarely in the eye, her face a mask of irony. 'Oh, please. Not that old line.'

It angered him. His hand stilled against her cheek. 'What a contrary creature you are.'

Nicky jumped to her feet. Beyond the fire, the book-lined shelves struck chill. But anything was better than sitting in that deceptive pool of light letting him mesmerise her.

She said pleasantly, 'And what a patronising rat you are.'

His dark brows twitched together sharply as if she had struck him. 'Rat? Why on earth…?'

But at least he sounded as if all his attention was back on what he was saying, not on some magic trap which she was not supposed to notice until it was too late. It was a relief.

'Think about it,' Nicky advised crisply from her safe haven in the shadows. 'Think about everything you've said to me since you arrived this evening.'

He stood up and came round the sofa. Not such a safe haven after all.

'What do you mean?' he demanded.

Nicky retreated a couple of steps.

'I was supposed to turn into the little woman and cook for you, while you dealt with your big important business deals, wasn't I?' she said breathlessly. If she stoked her anger at his behaviour this evening, she could suppress the older, darker memories. 'What did you call it? An evening as Mr Average?'

'I was wrong,' he said positively.

She backed. He followed. Nicky went on retreating, skirting a heavy oak table, bumping into a worn tapestry chair and nearly oversetting a set of library steps. Eventually there was only the long window at her back, with its skin-tingling draughts and the surge and thud of the sea beyond. And in front of her...

'Where are you going to run now?' Esteban challenged her provocatively.

Nicky gulped. 'I'm not running.'

One eyebrow rose. 'Aren't you?'

'No, of course not. But I should go and clear up...'

'Running,' he taunted softly.

Nicky's chin came up. He did not remember what she remembered after all. 'Why should I do that?' she retorted, challenging in her turn.

'Because you suspect I'm interested in you,' he said calmly. 'And you don't know how to handle it.'

Nicky stared at him blankly. He suddenly seemed very tall and much too close. His mouth smiled faintly. But the dark eyes were not amused.

'You're mad,' she said, shaken.

'Not at all. Though I'm surprised you're so unsure of yourself.'

That fired her up. 'I am not unsure of myself,' said Nicky between her teeth.

He ignored it. 'And of course you're right.' It was a purr. 'I am interested.'

Her indignation dwindled abruptly. His eyes travelled over her like a caress.

'The point is, are you?'

The silence shuddered with possibilities. Nicky's lips parted. Then she found she had nothing to say. She could only search his face, trying to read him.

A bit of her mind went scrabbling round on a hamster wheel that repeated frantically, Get out of this. Get out of this. Get out of this *now*. But another bit—a frighteningly calm bit—said, You've waited ten years for this. Go for it.

Nicky swallowed loudly.

The smooth voice roughened. 'Let's see, shall we?'

He reached for her.

It was not at all like ten years ago. For one thing he was—as he said he aimed to be—in total control. For another, Nicky was not fifteen and clumsy with the first anguish of sexual hunger.

To her surprise, his mouth was soft, questioning. Control, yes. But he explored without pressure as if he savoured every sensation. She had the feeling he registered every tiny quiver of response as her lips parted and, with a little sigh, she abandoned herself to the moment.

Her eyelids fluttered closed. She was floating. She heard herself give a muted sigh, half delight, half despair.

Esteban heard it too. His arms tightened bruisingly. Nicky surrendered. In his hands she felt impossibly slight, as if her body was a flimsy thing he could mould to his will. She drew a little breath of pure pleasure.

Suddenly urgent, his mouth ravaged hers. Oh, he was in control all right. Under his mastery her muscles turned to water and her bones became as flimsy as thistledown. For heady moments Nicky revelled in it.

Out of nowhere realisation struck her: *this was what it was like before*. It shocked her back to reason. She broke the kiss and leaned away from him, hands flat against his chest.

Esteban looked down at her as if he hardly recognised her. They were both panting.

'Nicky—' She hardly recognised the ragged voice.

What was more, she hardly recognised herself. Her blood was singing. For the first time since that night on the beach, she was not bracing herself to pretend that she was physically moved when she wasn't.

I can deal with this, thought Nicky in a flash of enlightenment. She could hardly believe it. *It's all right. I'm cured.* Off her guard with relief, she gave him a brilliant smile.

Esteban's eyes flared.

And that was when Nicky realised the danger she was in. Another of those searing kisses and she would be surrendering to his every last whim. Maybe even giving him the key to the memory he had not yet unlocked.

Shocked, she whipped out of his arms.

'No!'

His arms let her go. But his eyes, dark and intent, didn't. 'No? Why not?'

She could not tell him the truth. She searched desperately and found something that was halfway true.

'I don't want you experimenting with me.'

His eyes assessed her. She could almost see the acute brain working.

'I don't think you know what you want,' he said at last.

Nicky made a great business of looking at her watch.

'Well, I'm very tired.' She managed a huge and almost convincing yawn. 'I'll be asleep as soon as my head hits the pillow.'

His expression was shuttered. 'You don't have to draw me a diagram. Which room was made up for you?'

She described it.

'Ah,' he said.

For a moment, an unholy smile just touched the corners of his mouth. All Nicky's suspicions awoke again.

'What? What is it?'

He shook his head. 'Nothing. Just—'

But before he could finish what he was going to say the telephone on the windowsill rang. In pure reflex she reached for it at the same time as Esteban. Their hands collided.

There was an arc of energy. It shocked them both. Esteban's arm recoiled as if it burnt. His breath rasped, loud as a drumroll. Their eyes met. Nicky vibrated.

But she was the one with the telephone receiver in her hand. Shaken, she said, 'Hello?' in a voice so high and strained that she hardly recognised it.

Esteban watched, frowning.

There was as silence on the other end. Then a brittle voice said, 'I think I must have the wrong number. Who is that, please?'

Nicky checked the face of the old telephone and gave the number.

There was another pause. Then the voice queried, 'Hallam Hall?'

'Yes.' Too late Nicky realised that the voice was female and was obviously expecting to talk to Esteban. She said, her words falling over themselves in her confusion, 'Do you want to speak to Mr Tremain? He's right here. I'm sorry—'

But she was speaking to a buzzing line. The connection had been cut.

She looked across at Esteban. 'She's hung up. I'm sorry. That wasn't very bright of me.'

He did not seem as if he could be bothered to question her about it. 'No harm done.'

'But—she hung up.'

Esteban was impatient. 'Which means it can't have been very important. Now—we were talking about your room. Will you be warm enough?'

Nicky did not trust this sudden metamorphosis into a concerned host.

'I'll be fine,' she said firmly. 'In fact, I think I'll go to bed now. I've had a long drive today.' And she gave another huge yawn.

If she thought he would argue, she was disappointed.

'I'll say goodnight, then.'

He was waiting for her to go so he could call the woman who had hung up.

'Goodnight,' Nicky said distantly.

She went quickly through the corridors, not looking at the paintings. The dancing nymphs seemed to laugh after her as she hurried past them. It made her feel oddly bleak.

She hurried through a scrappy wash in the chilly bathroom and jumped into the four-poster bed. There were plenty of blankets. But the creaks and the draughts did not make it easy to go to sleep.

Nicky read as late as she could. When her eyelids were threatening to close of their own volition, she shut the book and turned off the light. But she could not relax, even though she was so tired.

She had never expected to confront Steve again, Nicky realised. He was a figure out of myth, haunting her yet distant. She had thought he was out of reach for ever. If she was honest, she had wanted him out of reach.

Now she was faced with the fact that he was a man, not a mythical monster. Not a kind man, maybe, but living flesh and blood. What was worse, the old pull was still there. In fact, it was stronger than ever.

'But so am I,' said Nicky aloud.

The problem was that Esteban was stronger too. More sophisticated, more controlled and all too acutely aware of the sexual tension between them. He might have forgotten that meeting on the beach ten years ago but he knew what had been happening tonight all right.

Nicky stared into the darkness and recognised an unwelcome truth.

If she was not very careful, it would all go the same way again.

CHAPTER SEVEN

SHE dreamed of cypress groves and a wild dance in which, for some reason, she was taking part covered in flour and not much else. The other girls laughed and did not seem to notice. But she was painfully conscious of her state of undress. Especially as she knew they were all waiting for the Lord of the Wood.

She had to get away before he looked and found her. She had to...

Nicky jackknifed into wakefulness, the dream still running. For all it was so silly it felt as if it carried a message of danger.

'Nicky?' She knew that soft voice.

Her sense of danger increased. For a crazy moment she lay there in the darkness, her heart thundering.

'Nicky.' Louder this time.

What had he said in the library? 'I am interested... The point is, are you?'

She thought, He's going to make me face my feelings. All my feelings. I'm not ready for this.

Her mouth dry, she hauled herself up on to her elbow, groping for the unfamiliar bedside light. But before she could find it the light snapped on. Nicky blinked.

Esteban was standing not in the doorway, as she had expected, but by the dressing table. The top drawer was open. And he was still fully dressed.

She cleared her throat. 'What are you doing?'

He pulled out a black box of some kind and slammed the drawer shut, turning to her.

'Just remembered something I wanted.'

Nicky huddled the heavy blankets up to her chin.

116

'What?' she said suspiciously.

'A torch.'

Nicky was blank. 'What do you want a torch for? And what's it doing in my room, anyway?'

Esteban hesitated. 'Sometimes the power goes off in old houses. It's always a good idea to have a torch at hand. And—er—it's my room, actually.'

Nicky was so shocked that she did not notice the evasiveness of the rest.

'*Your* room?' she echoed, disbelieving.

'Yes.'

Nicky forgot to clutch the blankets. Her hands twisted in agitation.

'But it was the only one made up. I thought it was for me.'

'Don't worry about it. You're very welcome.'

Nicky ignored that. 'You should have said,' she muttered.

She was torn between guilt and embarrassment at her suspicions. Even though he did not know what she had thought, she could feel the heat in her cheeks. She looked anywhere but at him.

'Why? Would you have offered to share?' His voice was amused. But there was a thread in it that had nothing at all to do with amusement.

And it demanded an answer.

Nicky lifted her head and met his eyes. There was a moment when the whole world seemed to hold its breath.

Then he said something—she thought it was her name— and cast the torch away as he strode forward. Dazed, Nicky let herself be swept up into his arms. She did not make even a token protest.

His hands were like fire. Through the creased cotton she wore, her traitorous body pressed wantonly against him. She was starkly aware of sheer male power. And even more starkly aware of her response to it.

Shocked and exhilarated, she opened her mouth to the invasion of his tongue. As hungry as he, she kicked away the tangled covers and reared against him. She was trembling with need.

Somewhere at the back of her mind, Nicky thought, *This is exactly the same as last time*. She did not care.

Esteban fell on to the bed, hauling her on top of him in a bone-crushing embrace. Nicky gave a small moan, half pain, half longing. Her breasts were hot and hard under the old nightdress. She writhed, hobbled by the twisted stuff. Esteban muttered in frustration. Nicky felt his breath hot in her mouth, his hands fierce.

And then the old cotton tore like paper.

Esteban lifted his mouth and flung her down among the tumbled covers. At once he began to slide down her body, his mouth hungry. Nicky screwed her eyes tight shut. The sensations were close to agony. But she thought she would die if he stopped.

'Say you want me.' His voice was muffled against her trembling flesh.

Nicky blenched. Her eyes flew open. This was facing her feelings with a vengeance. Could she do it?

Esteban felt her recoil. He looked up, his eyes black with desire. And dawning dismay.

'Don't you?' He sounded appalled.

Nicky swallowed.

'I—'

But she couldn't.

Esteban threw himself off the bed as if she had shot him. 'I think I'd better go.'

Nicky pressed her lips together so tightly they hurt. Her throat felt like sandpaper. She swallowed.

'I'm sorry,' she said in a voice she did not recognise.

'So am I,' he said curtly. 'Put it down to a difficult day. For both of us.'

'I should never—'

But he interrupted, his voice level. 'Nor should I. But there's no harm done.'

Oh, yes, there is, thought Nicky. Her every sensitised

nerve quivered, exactly as it had ten years ago. As it never had since. That revelation shocked her into wild alarm.

'Heaven help me.' Her voice spiralled upwards, on the edge of panic.

Esteban winced. Engrossed in her own self-betrayal, Nicky did not see it.

He said harshly, 'It's no big deal. Mistakes happen all the time.'

Nicky looked at him blankly. He made a quick, instinctive movement towards her. And curbed it as quickly. His dark face was quite unreadable.

'You'll find it will look different in the morning.'

And he picked up his torch and walked out.

For once things did not look better in the morning.

Nicky had spent a restless night, torn between listening to the slam of the sea on the rocks below and the disturbing dreams of half sleep. In the end, she gave up trying to sleep and got up as early as she decently could.

There was no sign of Esteban. Which was half a relief, half frustrating. Nicky shook her shoulders and refused to think about where he might be.

Instead she applied herself to the problems of the kitchen. She might not be able to replace all the fuses until the shops opened but at least she could find out which appliances needed them. Then she could be on her way back to London and out of Esteban's force field—and all it revealed of her own bewildering weakness.

She made herself a large mug of strong coffee and concentrated. If she kept her mind on her work, she reasoned, she would not have to think about last night. And if she could avoid thinking about it until she got back to the safety of her flat, then she had a sporting chance of looking Esteban in the eye before she left.

Work helped a bit. It took her a couple of hours to go round the kitchen thoroughly, pulling out units and wriggling behind machines. But in the end she was pretty sure she had the measure of the problem.

Not all the fuses had been removed. Sometimes the wiring had just been disconnected so there was no longer a circuit through the plug. Usually the wiring had been mutilated. Nicky had no doubt that the kitchen equipment had been sabotaged. By somebody who had plenty of time and was not afraid of being challenged if found in the kitchen. Somebody, she was pretty certain, whom Esteban Tremain knew.

She put in a call to Martin, reporting in. She knew he would be in the office early before he went to the exhibition hall.

'Hi. How's it going?' he said breezily. 'The girls have been worried about you. They thought you were going home this morning.'

'I was,' said Nicky. 'Something turned up.'

'Like what?' Martin asked, amused. It was an office joke that nothing diverted Nicky from her chosen path once she had made up her mind.

She took a deep breath. 'Our respected client.' Her tone of cynical unconcern was masterly. No one would guess she had been going mad in his arms last night.

'Esteban? That must have been a party and a half.'

Nicky shut her eyes, thanking heaven that Martin could not see her anguish.

'Offered my choice of companions for the evening, he would not be a hot favourite,' she said with careful irony.

And Martin suspected nothing.

She reported on the evening, editing heavily. Martin did not like the implications of any of it. His instructions were curt and businesslike.

'Put things right and get out pronto.'

Nicky was surprised at his tone. So surprised that she forgot that Martin was telling her to do exactly what she had already decided on.

'I don't think I'm in any danger, Martin. As Esteban said, it was just a silly trick.'

'Too silly. Whoever did it is not rational. And Hallam Hall is just too damned isolated.'

Perversely, Nicky objected. 'But I'm not alone. The client is here.'

Martin knew Hallam. 'My guess is that Esteban Tremain is working at the other end of the house. The Beast of Bodmin could come and tear you to bits in the kitchen and he wouldn't even hear the screams.'

Nicky shivered. There was a beast tearing her to bits, all right. Memory had a whole new set of claws after the way she had behaved last night.

'I'm not joking, Nicky. Do the business and get out.'

She knew it was the only sensible thing to do.

So she decided to take the car off to the nearest small town she could find on the map. She left a note for Esteban in the middle of the kitchen table.

She felt self-conscious, propping it up against her file. Something else that felt too intimate. But it was only practical to let him know that she had gone out.

Hell, she did not even know what to call him. She started the note four times: 'Mr Tremain… Dear Mr Tremain… Esteban… Dear Esteban…' None of them looked right.

In the end she did not head it at all, just scribbled it out as if she were in great hurry. 'Gone to get the fuses. Will bring back some bread and milk.' She signed it with the time she left and her initial. Nothing anyone could call personal there. She hoped Esteban would recognise it and behave accordingly.

The little market town was just about waking up when Nicky got there. A small ironmonger's proved to have the required fuses and replacement cable but the man serving her was not willing to surrender them until he knew where she had come from. Having extracted the information, he gave her a comprehensive run-down on Hallam Hall, its owner, Colonel Tremain, and how lucky he was to have a stepson like Mr Esteban.

'I'm sure,' said Nicky, acutely uncomfortable. She held out her hand for her change.

'He works hard, Mr Esteban,' said the shop man, not handing it over. 'You'd think he wouldn't need to bother—his real dad being a millionaire and all.'

He paused invitingly. But Nicky was almost dancing with discomfort.

'I wouldn't know,' she said curtly. 'I just work there. Good morning.'

She seized her change and ran.

The baker's shop was no different—though she learned there that Mr Esteban was a very fair employer, even though everyone had been worried when he'd taken over running the farm from the Colonel—and the woman in the small general provisions store virtually barred Nicky's exit while she told her every daring exploit that Mr Esteban had been up to since he'd first arrived at Hallam at the age of eleven.

Nicky felt as if everyone in the single street was watching her as she made her way back to the car. It was all she could do not to run the last few yards. She did run into the kitchen when she finally got back to the Hall.

'Phew,' she said, pulling off a headscarf and shaking out her damp blonde hair.

Esteban Tremain was at the kitchen table reading a newspaper and drinking coffee. Nicky stopped dead when she saw him. It was like walking into a waterfall. At once every idea roared out of her, leaving only the memory of last night's turbulence. And dread.

Esteban looked up. His expression was unreadable. Nicky's mouth dried.

Was he going to reproach her? Demand an explanation? Touch her? Wild images shot across her brain. She stood, frozen, in the middle of the kitchen floor.

He lowered the paper slowly.

'How are you?'

Nicky swallowed. 'Soaked,' she said, taking refuge in briskness.

He studied her searchingly. 'That's all?'

She turned away, tossing her shopping on to the dresser.

'Well, I feel I've just run the gauntlet.'

'Local people are always very interested in what happens at Hallam.' He was still watching her.

As if he expected her to burst into flames or start throwing things, she thought. She forced a laugh.

'Interested! I think I've had your life story.'

He folded up the newspaper and stood up. 'Nicky—'

She rushed into speech, not looking at him.

'I'll replace all these fuses. Then make sure that everything's working.' She was gabbling. 'After that I'll be on my way.'

He stood very still. 'Is that what you want?'

She risked a glance at him then.

'I think it would be sensible.'

Esteban looked at her gravely.

'Are you always sensible?'

Nicky was full of self-mockery. 'Usually.'

Except with him.

'Then maybe it's time for a change,' Esteban suggested softly.

He was not touching her. He was not anywhere near her. But the energy beating out of him forced her to look at him. Nicky found she was actually tilting backwards in a physical effort to resist.

'Don't you think we have things to talk about?'

Panic flared, swift as a forest fire. Did he suspect they had met before? Had he, too, started to remember a night on a Caribbean beach?

'No,' said Nicky forcefully.

Oh, no, it would not be sensible to stay. It would be crazy.

Nicky broke that mesmeric eye contact and said woodenly, 'No, I'd rather get back. I have a lot of work to do.'

There was a long silence. Nicky turned her head away. She could feel his eyes on her profile, but he did not ask any dangerous questions. And he did not try to persuade her.

'Shame,' he said at last.

She thought, He doesn't really care.

Which, she assured herself, was exactly what she wanted. Wasn't it?

Esteban turned away, picking up his car keys. 'Will you be all right if I leave you to get on with it, then? I have to see my stepfather.'

'I'll be fine.'

On his way out of the door, he paused. 'Will you be here when I get back?' He could not have sounded less interested.

'If you get back before I've finished the kitchen,' she said pleasantly.

'I see.'

She thought he would leave then but he did not. Instead he surveyed the keys for a moment, then looked across at her very directly.

'What has sent you into retreat, Nicky? Village gossip?'

Nicky gave a false little laugh. 'I don't know what you're talking about.'

'No?' He patently did not believe her. 'Have it your own way.' He shrugged, turning away. 'I'll be back in a couple of hours. If you leave before I get back, lock up but don't bother about the burglar alarm.'

He left. Nicky felt bereft. She flung herself at the machines.

Putting the fuses back and then restoring the kitchen to its former state took longer than Nicky had expected. In the end she found she would need to touch up some of the paintwork and even replace a couple of tiles. A quick call to the local installers told her where the spare materials had been left. She rooted them out from the cupboard off the pantry and made the repairs.

All the time, she worked with an ear alert for the sound of Esteban's Jaguar. It did not come. At last she could not convince herself that there was anything more for her to do. She packed up her files, stuffed her few clothes back into her overnight bag and loaded both into her car.

She left a brief, neutral note for Esteban on Springdown headed paper. Then locked the mighty wooden door and climbed into the car. There was a strong wind off the sea which made the car rock. But it was not that which made her shiver convulsively as she settled behind the wheel.

She would have given almost anything not to be setting off, Nicky realised. The drive was long. The autumn day was already starting to darken. The wind shook the car. And she would probably never see Esteban Tremain again.

'Stop it,' Nicky said aloud to herself. 'You did not succumb to his charm and he still doesn't know you've met before. You've got away with your tail feathers. Be grateful. And drive.'

The car started easily, drove for about sixty seconds and then rolled gently to a halt as if it had run out of petrol. Nicky checked the fuel gauge. No, it was more than half full. She tried the ignition again. The engine flickered into life and died.

She got out. The car had got her out of the lee of the Hall and the wind made her stagger. Nicky set her teeth and had a look under the bonnet. Everything looked normal. But then how would I know if it wasn't normal? Nicky thought in self-disgust. She felt inadequate and it infuriated her.

'Blonde,' she said aloud furiously.

She could have cried. Or pushed the thing into the sea. Instead she contented herself with kicking a tyre viciously. Then she trudged back to the Hall.

Esteban was still not back. Nicky tried to tell herself that it was a relief. This way she might be able to contact someone to tow the car away and take her to the station before he returned. So she would not have to see him again. Which was what she wanted. Wasn't it?

She found a telephone directory in the study. It was easy to identify the nearest garage. The man who answered was frustratingly unhelpful until she mentioned that she was staying at Hallam Hall.

'Tell Mr Esteban I'll be out as soon as I can,' he said,

ringing off before Nicky could point out that the car in question was hers.

And then she heard the sound of a powerful car's wheels on the gravel. Slowly, she put down the phone.

It had to be Esteban. Her heart leapt.

Nicky shook her head. This was no good. She squared her shoulders, did some deep breathing, and went to the kitchen.

He was standing at the kitchen table, head bent, reading the paper in his hand. Nicky realised that it was her note. She cleared her throat.

Esteban looked up. She saw that his brows were knotted in a fierce frown. He regarded her blackly for a few unspeaking moments, almost as if he did not believe it.

'I thought you'd gone.'

'I had.' For some reason her voice was thready. She moistened her lips.

The black frown did not lighten but a little flame lit in the depths of those dark eyes.

'What made you change your mind?'

'I—'

He did not move a muscle but she felt as if he had come towards her. As if he was reaching for her.

'Decided to have a go at not being sensible after all?' he suggested softly.

For a crazy moment Nicky was tempted to say yes. To take the two steps that would take her to him and see what happened. *Be sensible,* she told herself.

'My car,' she managed.

'Ah. Of course.' His frown disappeared. So did the little flame. 'I should have expected it. We are haunted by mechanical disasters. What's wrong?'

'It stopped.'

'Well, that's pretty final,' he agreed.

He gave her a lazy smile. Nicky knew it should have charmed her to bits. Instead it was oddly chilling.

'It won't start. I don't know why. The petrol is all right. I need a mechanic.'

'Did you leave your lights on?'

Nicky had had a hard day and she was coming close to the end of her endurance as far as this man was concerned.

'Oh, isn't that just typical?' she flashed. 'Is that what blondes do? Run their batteries down because they're too fluffy-headed to remember to turn their lights off?'

Esteban shrugged. 'Anyone can forget they've got their lights on. Especially on grey days like these.'

'Well, I didn't.' Nicky was still fulminating. 'You think I'm a complete bimbo, don't you?'

Esteban shook his head. 'Whenever did I say that?'

Put on the spot, of course, Nicky could not remember. Except—

'You called me a *blonde*!' She did a savage imitation of his dismissive tone on the telephone.

He stared at her incredulously.

'Is that what this is all about?'

Nicky stared at him with hot eyes. 'All what?'

'This morning. When you wouldn't talk.'

'I talked—'

'Last night,' he went on as if she had not spoken. 'When we nearly made love.' He paused, then added deliberately, 'Should have made love.'

It was the last thing Nicky expected.

'You're out of your mind,' she said when she could speak.

He considered that dispassionately. 'You could be right. I thought that the moment I walked out on you last night.'

The old feelings of vulnerability washed over her like a tidal wave, drowning every other sensation. She felt adrift; helpless. For a moment she hated him.

Esteban saw it. His eyes widened. He looked shocked.

'What *is* it?'

Nicky whipped round and almost ran to the sink. She ran her hands under the tap, lathering them recklessly with washing-up liquid.

'I got grease all over me.' She was talking at random, breathless. Esteban came up behind her.

'I never meant to upset you.'

He brushed the drifting hairs off her neck, where they had fallen out of the knot she had skewered on top of her head. Nicky froze.

'Of course you're blonde.' His voice was husky. 'Blonde and beautiful.'

'Don't.' It was hardly more than a breath.

She could feel his eyes on her.

'Don't what? Tell you you're beautiful? Or kiss your neck?'

Nicky stood like a statue. She felt his breath against the exposed skin of her neck. Or she thought she did. She quivered. A thought came: I've been waiting for this for ten years.

He brushed the nape of her neck with his fingertips. Nicky let out a strangled breath.

'Well,' he said in an odd voice.

She did not turn round.

'If you touch me again,' she said harshly to Martin's finely crafted plate racks, 'I shall call a cab to Exeter and go now. I don't care about leaving the car. I can get the train or stay in a hotel or—' Her voice became suspended.

He turned her round to face him. His arms were strong. There was nowhere to go.

'This is nonsense,' Esteban said harshly.

And kissed her.

Against her will, against every consideration of common sense and her own decision, Nicky kissed him back. Her kiss held all the fire of anger, all the desperation of last night's self-betrayal. When they fell apart they were both panting.

He stared at her as if he had never seen her before. Or, rather, as if he had suddenly realised that she was somebody quite other than the person he had thought.

He's remembered! thought Nicky, horrified.

'Don't look like that!' he shouted.

She jumped.

'I'm sorry,' he said in a more moderate tone. 'But you

keep looking at me as if you think I'll hurt you. I don't like it.'

'Then don't give me cause,' retorted Nicky.

She pushed past him. The kiss had shaken her more than anything that had gone before.

He gave a laugh that was half a groan. '*What* cause? And don't give me any nonsense about calling you a blonde. You must have got used to the idea after all these years.'

Oh, God, he *had* remembered. Nicky felt sick.

'What years? What do you mean?' she said sharply.

'Even if you don't believe your mirror,' he said judicially, 'your lovers must have told you how beautiful you are.'

The mockery was unexpected, and so cruel that Nicky could have screamed. Then she saw the look in his eyes. Unbelieving, she realised he was perfectly serious. Oh, boy, am I out of my depth, she thought.

But all she said was, 'N-no.'

He did not touch her. But the way he looked at her was a potent caress.

'Then let me be the first,' he said softly.

There was a deafening silence. Out of my depth and drowning, Nicky thought.

They just stood looking at each other, not moving. It might have been an hour; it might have been a few seconds. Nicky felt the steady floor shift under her as if it were preparing for an earthquake. She put an uncertain hand behind her and grasped the countertop.

'From the first time I saw you,' Esteban said at last.

Nicky could have wept. 'You don't even remember the first time you saw me,' she said bitterly.

'Oh, but I do. Across a floor full of fridges.' He gave a soft laugh. 'Hardly romantic. You'd come in from the street and your hair was all blown about.'

He touched the hair at her temples gently. She was so stunned she did not retreat.

'All gold, like the summer.'

Nicky felt his hands loosening the pins that held her knot

in place. She did not resist. The pins clattered on to the flag-stones. Her hair slid down over his fingers. To her amazement, it felt voluptuous as velvet as it flowed over his skin. She shook it out deliberately, so that it caressed his fingers. Heard his little indrawn gasp of pleasure. Leaned into him…

This time the kiss was long and slow. Half a question, half a promise of passion. The passion was unmistakable, thought Nicky, who had avoided passion for years. Until last night. She was deeply shaken by her certainty. Especially as she was almost sure Esteban shared it.

His eyes were intense. 'At least now you know I wasn't making fun of you.'

Nicky shook her head, dazed and trembling. No, he was not making fun of her. He was starting to make love to her again. His sort of love, not hers. But she did not think she could resist.

She said as she had said last night, 'Oh, heaven help me.' She hardly knew she was speaking aloud.

Esteban shook her slightly. 'Stop fighting it,' he murmured. 'You know you need this as much as I do.'

And the trouble was, she *did*. She did not know which was worse—the way she despised herself or the sexy confidence in Esteban's eyes.

He slid a hand round the back of her waist under the grubby shirt and ran a mischievous finger down her spine. Nicky could not suppress the bolt of sensation which shot through her. His eyes gleamed with triumph.

'We'll call the garage tomorrow,' he said roughly, preparing to swing her up into his arms.

At that moment Nicky did, literally, hate him. Nobody should be that sure of another human being.

She pushed him away and strengthened her wavering backbone. 'Too late. I've already called. They said they'd be here as soon as possible.'

Esteban groaned.

But when the man arrived Esteban was courtesy itself. He

made him coffee before taking him out to the beached car.
To small effect.

The dungareed St George took one look at Nicky's car and
shook his head. In spite of Esteban's objections, he insisted
on escorting her back to the car for diagnosis. Esteban slipped
an oversized waxed jacket over Nicky's clothes and accompanied them, one arm protectively round her.

'You won't get that started,' said the garage man with
gloomy relish.

Nicky was suspicious. Had Esteban slipped him a bribe to
claim her car was beyond repair tonight?

'How can you tell?' she demanded. 'You haven't even
looked inside the engine.'

The man traced the edge of the fuel cap with his finger.
'See that?'

Nicky leaned closer. It looked as if there was some sort of
gritty discharge from it. She touched it. The crystals felt
sticky.

'What is it?'

'Sugar.'

Esteban, who had been watching with detached interest,
suddenly lost his detachment. He leaned forward.

'What? Joe, that has to be nonsense.'

The man stood back. 'See for yourself.'

Esteban did, frowning.

'But how could sugar have got into the petrol?' Nicky said,
puzzled. 'And why?'

'Gums up the pipes,' said Joe laconically. 'Sugar doesn't
dissolve in oil, you see. Just forms into a mass and stops the
petrol flowing. Bet you thought you'd run out.'

'But how can it have got into the tank?'

'Only one way. Someone put it there.'

Esteban said, 'But that means someone deliberately—'

'Sabotage,' said Nicky shakily. 'Again.' She felt a cold
which had nothing to do with the wind buffeting them off
the sea.

Esteban looked down at her in quick concern. 'Well, vandalism, certainly. Can you do anything about it, Joe?'

'Needs to be stripped down. I'll take it back and see what I can do.'

Esteban took the keys from Nicky's nerveless hand and passed them across.

'Do that. Let us know how it looks. Put it on the Hall's account.'

Nicky came out of her shocked reverie. 'I can pay for it. I've got my credit card.'

Esteban put his arm round her again. The gale made them both stagger and whipped her hair across her mouth. He brushed it gently behind her ear.

'We'll talk about it later. Let Joe see what's wrong first.' He hugged her comfortingly. 'Go back. You're frozen.'

She turned to him instinctively. His body was warm. His strength seemed to revive and sustain her. Nicky felt herself steadied.

'Yes,' she said thankfully.

He gave her a little push. 'Go and get warm. I'll just help Joe hitch up your car.'

'My case—'

'I'll bring it in,' he assured her. 'Go on.'

She went.

After about ten minutes Esteban followed. He took one look at her white face and came over to her.

'Don't look so worried.'

'What was it you were saying about your enemies?' Nicky said. 'Is sugar in the petrol tank their sort of form?'

His eyes did not quite meet hers. 'Much too childish.'

She huddled her arms round herself, although the kitchen was warm as toast.

'But effective.'

'Only in the short run.'

He reached out but Nicky drew away. A thought had occurred to her and she needed an answer.

'Is that what you were doing in my room last night?'

His eyes narrowed. 'What?'

She was seeing him standing at the dressing table, still fully dressed. He had not come bent on seduction, had he? She had just jumped to that conclusion. And then let her long-repressed hunger take over.

'You really were looking for a torch, weren't you?'

Esteban watched her. 'I told you I was.'

And she had just brushed it side. Nicky's whole body burned with shame. She tried to ignore it.

'What happened?' Her voice was harsh. 'Did you hear an intruder?'

He seemed to debate with himself. Then he shrugged.

'I wasn't sure. I thought I'd take a look. Only then—' his voice warmed to sexy amusement '—something came up that seemed more urgent.'

He slanted a look at her. It said as clearly as words that he enjoyed the memory. It invited her to share his pleasure. Nicky winced.

'And did you find anything? I mean—' she swallowed painfully '—afterwards.'

The amusement died out of his face. 'Nothing definite.'

'Have you told the police?'

'Until now there was nothing to tell.'

She looked round the kitchen, at all the machines she had spent the day rewiring.

'Wasn't there?' she said heavily.

His jaw tightened. 'Nothing I couldn't handle.'

Nicky shivered, not answering.

His voice gentled. 'Look, Nicky, I know this feels bad. But I'm almost sure you were right when you said it was all my own fault. So I'll deal with it.'

'Great,' muttered Nicky. 'Like you'll beam in a new engine for my car?'

'I can't do that,' Esteban admitted, his mouth wry. 'But I can take care of everything else.' His eyes compelled her to look at him. 'Believe me,' he said with great deliberation, 'I will take care of you.'

All Nicky's memories attacked. Miserably undecided, she wrung her hands.

'Trust me,' he said strongly.

What choice did she have? For tonight, at least, she was stuck. In the end she admitted it, at least to herself.

'All right,' she said reluctantly.

Esteban's mouth turned down as if he had bitten on something sour.

'I'll make you forget all this,' he vowed.

Nicky thought of all she had to forget. More than he knew.

'You can try.'

From his alert glance, she knew he'd registered her reservations. But he was too shrewd to challenge her.

Instead he said lightly, 'Why don't you go and have one of your scented baths? I'll make a few phone calls, then I'll give you the guided tour. And later I'll take you out for a meal. That will put everything into perspective.'

Nicky very much doubted it. On the other hand, a bath would be very welcome. She agreed.

Later she came downstairs in her last remaining change of clothes: sapphire velvet trousers and a softly alluring sweater the colour of cornflowers. It made her skin look porcelain and turned her eyes sea blue. Esteban, coming out of the study, stopped dead.

'You beautiful thing,' he said after a stunned pause. He sounded almost angry.

Nicky's chin lifted to a challenging angle. 'So?'

He stared at her for a moment, his eyes hot.

'What is it you're not telling me?'

Nicky jumped, disconcerted. 'You're imagining it.'

'Am I?' He was grim. 'You know we want each other. You feel it, just like I do. But then you remember something and you turn on me as if I'm your enemy. Last night—' He broke off with a frustrated, furious gesture. 'Why?'

Nicky should have told him then. She knew she should have told him. She could not bear it.

She said in a high, tense voice, 'I thought you were going to show me round the house.'

He gave an exasperated exclamation. But Nicky was already turning away. Esteban shrugged and followed.

He took her from room to room like a professional guide. Except that no professional would have loved the place as he clearly did, treated it so carelessly and yet with such affection. He seemed to know the history of every stick of furniture, every tapestry, every fireplace. But it was on the paintings that he really came into his own.

'School of Botticelli,' he would say. Or, 'Tintoretto. The insurance is ruinous.' Or again, 'Van Dyck. A rather badly behaved ancestor, I'm afraid, but a nice picture.' Eventually he stopped in front of three garlanded girls in a midsummer copse. 'Raphael, according to my stepfather. Fortunately the experts don't agree with him or we wouldn't be able to afford the security.'

Nicky looked at the laughing girls. She felt hot and cold. Hot with embarrassment to be standing beside Esteban looking at all that luxuriant abandon. Cold with dread that she would never be able to throw off her inhibitions and dance in the sun.

Esteban frowned. 'One of them will have to be sold, though. I don't know how my stepfather will bear it.'

Nicky was struck. 'How odd. My parents regard all possessions as goods for barter.'

He looked down at her. 'Don't they have things they treasure? Think of as part of the family?'

Nicky laughed aloud at the thought. 'My parents? You're joking.'

'I don't mean a painting, necessarily. Something they inherited from their parents that stands for continuity.'

'Let me tell you about my parents,' Nicky said, glad of the diversion. 'They're the original flower children. Flowers don't make good heirlooms.'

He was taken aback. 'Flower children? And *you*?'

Nicky grinned suddenly. 'Peace and love, man. My upbringing in a nutshell. My parents are the last hippies. They made the Summer of Love last thirty years. So far.'

'So you're a rebel against parental conditioning?'

'I think I must be,' Nicky said reflectively.

She looked at all the voluptuous flesh on the canvas over her head. Constraint returned, sharp as a wind off the sea. She looked at her watch.

'When are we eating?'

Esteban looked from Nicky to the painting; and back.

'Ah,' he said, as if he understood everything suddenly.

He lent her the oversized waxed jacket again and put her into the low, gleaming Jaguar. The wind howled but the car seemed impervious to its buffeting. Esteban set it silently down the darkened lanes to a sprawling inn at a crossroads.

The restaurant was a tiny room, with just five tables. Every one of them was full in spite of it being midweek and long past the tourist season. And from the moment they stepped inside Nicky felt as if they were alone.

Alone and—she drew a wondering breath—in love. All her prickly anger had gone. Their discreet corner table was like a charmed place, where nothing existed but the candlelight and each other. Even the waiter hardly impinged on Nicky's consciousness. She was quite calm and she had total confidence that Esteban would bring the evening to the resolution that had been waiting for them since they were born.

He looked steadily at her across the flame as if he could see right down into her soul.

'Tell me about these flower-children parents.'

She did. For the first time she found herself laughing about the trials of life on a boat, instead of denying them.

'It sounds a tough childhood.'

'Well, my brother had the time of his life,' Nicky said fairly. 'For myself, I could probably have done with a bit more structure.'

'I sail a lot,' observed Esteban, 'and I love it. But I can't imagine living on a boat permanently. What did you do for privacy?'

He leaned forward, as if he really needed to know. Under his intense regard, Nicky began to feel slightly light-headed.

'Lived without it,' she said breathlessly.

She felt oddly detached, almost as if she were in a trance. That it did not matter what they said—it was their eyes that were talking.

'That can't have been easy when you were growing up.'

She watched his mouth. It was a beautiful mouth, sculpted and strong. Here, you would say, was a deeply sensual man with his desires under rigid control. She wanted to touch his mouth. She wanted to see what would breach that iron control.

She tried to concentrate on the conversation. 'Living on a boat, you tend to make your mistakes in public. Growing up was not easy. But it was fast.'

He reached round the candle and took her hand. Nicky gave a sweet, deep shiver. Esteban saw it. His eyes darkened.

And then the waiter came, bringing food. Unhurried, Esteban let her hand go and sat back, allowing the man to serve. But his eyes never left her face.

Nicky knew it. If Andrew Bolton or any other man had looked at her with such unrelenting scrutiny she would have run for cover. But in her trance-like state she gloried in it. She thought, I want him to look at me like that for ever.

They ate. They talked, though Nicky could hardly have said what it was about. And all the time he looked at her as if they were alone.

Esteban seemed as if he wanted to tell her everything about himself. He talked about his work, his travels, his sailing; about his stepfather—with affection—and, with a brevity that revealed how painful it was, his real father. 'Do you see him?'

'Not much,' he said curtly.

Nicky was so sensitised to Esteban this evening that she knew the matter could not be allowed to rest there.

'Why not?' she asked gently.

He looked into the candle flame. 'The truth, if you must

have it, is that Felipe has been trying to mend bridges ever
since I was eighteen. I'm his only son and he takes that
seriously. For a long time I would not see him at all. But
then my mother died and the loyalties became less clear.
So—we meet occasionally.'

'And why does that hurt?'

But he made a sharp, dismissive gesture and the subject
was closed.

It was a shock, after their mutual openness. Nicky's calm
confidence dimmed a little. She retreated, grew more polite,
less spontaneous.

Esteban noted it ruefully. He called for the bill.

But in the car intimacy reasserted itself, silently. The stars
were needle-bright behind the surging clouds. It made Nicky
giddy to look at the sky. When the car came to that rise in
the road, it looked as if they were going to drive off the cliff
into the stars. She gasped and held on to her seat in pure
instinct.

Esteban sent her a quick look.

He said abruptly, 'Look, I'll tell you why I avoid Felipe.'

Nicky waited. Esteban brought the car to a halt. She could
sense him marshalling his words. Fluent and sophisticated
though he was, he found this hard to say, she realised. They
sat in silence for a moment under the wheeling stars.

Eventually he went on in a low voice, as if it was being
torn out of him, 'My mother was terrified of Felipe in the
end. He was passionate about her but he did not trust her.
He did not trust her *because* he was passionate about her.'

The intensity of it shook her. She did not know what to
say.

'Everything she did made him jealous. The whole thing
was insane.'

Nicky swallowed. 'So she ran away with your stepfather
and everything ended happily. Why should you blame yourself?'

Esteban gave a short laugh. 'You're missing the point. I'm
my father's son.'

Nicky was bewildered. 'So?'

'They even call me the Latin Lover in chambers. They think it's a joke, of course.'

She winced, remembering. 'Señoritas fall over themselves for that Latin charm,' Piers had said. And she had fallen all right, hadn't she? She shut her eyes.

Esteban did not notice her withdrawal. He was deep in a blackness of his own. 'Given the right circumstances, I could do what he did.' His voice was raw with self-loathing.

Nicky's eyes flew open. She could not have been more shocked if he had got out of the car and tipped her over the cliff into the sea.

'What?'

He was looking directly ahead but she had an uncomfortable feeling that it was not the landscape he was looking at. For a long moment he did not speak. Then he gave a deep sigh and put the car in gear again. It slipped along the narrow lane in near silence.

'I've always known what I was capable of,' he said at last sombrely.

She forgot her own bad memories in the need to defuse the nightmare for him. But how? In the end she chose scorn.

'You mean you think you are some sort of clone of your father? P-lease.'

He smiled perfunctorily. 'No, not that. But that if I let myself care deeply for someone—if I stopped watching myself—I could go wild. Lose all control.'

In spite of her determined common sense, Nicky shivered at his words. It was quite clear that Esteban Tremain believed them.

'And have you ever? Lost it, I mean.'

He hesitated. She had a feeling there was something burning inside him that, even now, he could not bear to expose.

In the end it was almost inaudible. 'Only once.'

CHAPTER EIGHT

HALLAM HALL was black and massive as the Jaguar's powerful headlights raked the sky. Esteban brought the car to a halt outside the studded door and sat for a moment. Nicky looked at him uneasily.

'What is it?'

'Maybe nothing.'

But when he opened the Gothic door and reached for the light switch nothing happened. Nicky gave a small gasp. It felt like a scream. At once his arm came round her, steadying her.

'It's all right. I told you the power goes off sometimes.'

But they had been too close tonight and he could no longer deceive Nicky with a reassuring tone. She knew it was not all right.

Keeping his arm round her, Esteban felt along a shelf. There was a click. A powerful beam scanned the hallway. It was empty.

It seemed to her that some tension in Esteban relaxed. But all he said was, 'I'll give you a candle.'

He found one, already set up in an incongruous old tin holder. He lit it and gave it to her. The flame shook as Nicky took hold of it. She tried to control her shaking.

'There you are. You can go to bed without breaking your neck now,' he said lightly. 'I'll just take a look round.'

She lifted the candle to search his expression. 'What is going on, Esteban?'

The candle had set all the shadows alive. They made Esteban's face unreadable.

'Don't tell me it's nothing,' said Nicky strongly. 'I mended those plugs, remember.'

'And you should remember that I said I'd take care of you,' he told her.

He looked down at her. In the crazy light, his face was a dramatic mask of planes and hollows. Nicky held her candle higher. Suddenly, his mouth was brilliantly illuminated. It was a long, curling mouth, devastating in its sensuality.

Nicky's stomach turned over. At once he pointed the candle away from his face and picked her up. Nicky gave a small scream and clutched at him to save herself from falling. The candle flame flared wildly.

'What are you *doing*?'

'Taking care of you,' he said.

He shouldered his way past various tables and chests to the foot of the tapestry-hung staircase. Nicky held the candle straight out ahead of them, in case one of the thousand draughts blew the wavering flame on to his skin or hers. It made the shadows dance.

'You're crazy,' she said with conviction. 'Put me down.'

'Are you or are you not scared?'

At once Nicky fired up. 'Don't you start cross-examining me. Of course I'm scared. That doesn't me I want you to carry mean to bed...'

The moment the words were out of her mouth she wished she had said anything else. Esteban stopped at the foot of the staircase. He did not say anything. In the darkness Nicky felt her face heat. She could have screamed.

'*Damn.* I didn't mean...'

Esteban put her down. He did not let her go, though. She stood in the iron circle of his arms, effectively his prisoner.

'You mean you *do* want me to carry you to bed?'

Nicky jumped. It sent the reflection of the candle flame leaping all round the walls. Esteban removed one arm from her waist and steadied the taper.

'Nicky, are you scared of me?' he said softly.

Nicky felt suddenly breathless.

'Don't be ridiculous.'

'Then scared of me forgetting myself and doing all the things you don't want?'

Nicky did not know what she wanted. She stood very still, her thoughts whirling. In the restaurant she had wanted quite passionately to touch and be touched. She had even revelled in the way he looked at her; wanted more. Now—

Now constraint froze her muscles, as deadly as snake venom. She could not answer.

'I know.' Esteban touched her hair briefly, as if he could not help himself. Then he stood back, letting her go. 'Go to bed,' he said quietly. 'You'll be quite safe. I promise.'

He was not talking about people who sabotaged kitchens and they both knew it.

Nicky hugged her candle and ran up the stairs to her room. The pictured nymphs flared briefly into life as the candle raced past them. They seemed to mock her.

Nicky undressed but she did not go to bed. She blew out the candle and prowled her room in the moonlight. Her thoughts were in turmoil.

Even though she could not see it in the dark, she was conscious of the photograph on the chest. It seemed to glare at her accusingly. She ought to tell Esteban that they had met before. Even if he did not remember that night, he had the right to know that she did. She must be giving him so many conflicting messages. He had asked her *why*. He had the right to an answer.

Face it, she thought. You keep saying that you want to get away as fast as you can. But you grab every excuse you can find to stay right here. There is something between you and Esteban Tremain. Maybe it's unfinished business. Maybe it isn't. Either way, you aren't going to find out until you tell him.

Outside in the corridor there was a series of creaks, then a thud. Nicky stood still, ears straining. Without the central heating, the natural chill of the castle reasserted itself. She shivered, pulling her dressing gown tight round her. There was a loud crash, a series of thumps, angry voices...

She gasped, *'Esteban,'* and rushed out into the corridor.

From the end of the passage came the sound of steady cursing. A strong torch beam flooded the carved ceiling. The torch itself had ended up against a Chinese urn. On the other side of the corridor a crouched figure held his elbow against his chest and swore fluently. Nicky ran forward.

'What is it? What happened?'

Esteban picked himself up from the ruptured rug.

'He got away,' he said bitterly.

Nicky picked up the torch and gave it to him.

'Who was it?'

'I don't know.' He sounded grim. 'Not the person I expected, certainly.'

From outside they heard the sound of an engine firing like a rocket.

'Motorbike,' diagnosed Esteban. 'He must have left it out of sight.'

Nicky shivered. 'He must have been in the house when we got back. Are you going to call the police *now*?'

'I suppose I'll have to.' He did not sound very enthusiastic about it.

She clutched his arm. 'Don't go after him yourself.'

He looked surprised. 'It's all right. I'll just—'

Nicky was shaking. 'Don't.'

Esteban put a strong hand over hers. 'Darling, it's all right,' he said soothingly. 'He's gone. I couldn't catch him even if I tried. I was just going to check the door is bolted and then reset the alarm.'

But Nicky would not let him go alone. She despised timid women and she did not exactly cling to his arm while he checked the doors. But she did not move far from his side, either. And when he went into the library to put in the call to a bored police constable she hovered so close that she bumped into his injured arm.

He gave a sharp exclamation and rubbed his elbow.

'What? Oh, no, sorry, Greg. My house guest just reminded me I've got a few bruises.'

The police constable became a lot less bored. Nicky approved but Esteban laughed at him.

'No, the man didn't hit me. We fell over each other, that's all. He's probably got as many bruises as I have. I'm more worried about what might be missing. I haven't found anything yet but we've got no power at the moment so I can't be sure.'

The loss of power interested the constable even more. Sighing, Esteban agreed that the police could come over the following morning.

He put the phone down and stirred the blackened log that was all that remained of the earlier fire. The embers glowed red and he flung on another log. A small flame caught. He turned briefly to Nicky.

'They want to see you too, I'm afraid. It looks like you'll have to spend another day here.' He kicked the log and added another two or three, not looking at her. 'You must think you're never going to get away from me.'

The fire was catching fast now. The flames crackled, leaping high in the old fireplace. Esteban stared at the flames broodingly.

'No,' she said in a strange voice.

Esteban looked at her quickly. 'Are you all right?'

Nicky hesitated. No, of course she wasn't all right. She had been terrified for him. Even now that he was safe her heart was beating so hard that it hurt.

She said harshly, 'I don't want to spend the night alone.'

For a moment there was a blank silence. The burning wood fizzed and chattered but the man hardly seemed to be breathing. Nicky cleared her throat loudly.

'I said—'

'I heard what you said.' His voice was rough. 'Is it post-intruder panic or do you mean it?'

Her heart galloped. Did she? She found she was holding her breath.

Esteban said softly, 'Nicky?'

She let out her breath with a great whoosh. It sounded like a sob.

He took her hands swiftly into his. She was shivering, not just with cold or reaction. When he touched her, she shivered harder.

'I mean it,' she whispered.

In the fight his shirt had ripped at the shoulder seam, so it fell from his waistband like a rag. Nicky saw his ribs rising and falling. The beam of the torch illuminated it like a spotlight. He was breathing hard. His chest was warm. Nicky twisted one of her hands gently out of his grasp and brushed her fingertips against the naked skin. His breathing stopped.

'Nicky,' he said in a strangled voice.

And then, quite suddenly, she stopped shaking. She felt like his powerful car, suddenly finding the right gear after labouring horribly uphill. She felt calm and clear-headed. The only thing she needed to make her fly was Esteban.

She thought, in faint surprise, I want him. Only him. He is the only one I have ever wanted. Why didn't I realise that?

She leaned forward and pressed her lips against the base of his throat.

Esteban was breathing again, carefully. 'Is this sensible?' he said, shaken.

His skin tasted of wine and wood smoke. Irresistible, thought Nicky, all her senses heightened. It made her light-headed. She felt suddenly, gloriously irresponsible.

'Who wants sensible?' she murmured.

'I thought you did,' he said on a flicker of amusement, though his mouth twisted as if he was in pain. He did not touch her. 'Didn't we agree that we both needed to stay in control?'

'So?'

He held her away from him. 'God knows I want you. But, Nicky, what good can come from two control freaks making love?' It sounded as if it hurt him to say it.

If you're going to break the habit of a lifetime, go for gold,

Nicky thought. There's no point in going slightly out of character. Turn Miss Prim on her head.

Quite deliberately she moved her mouth down his ribcage, savouring each sensuous touch, each spasm of reaction which he could not disguise.

'Broaden our horizons,' she said brazenly.

She loosened the sash of her old dressing gown. The shirt that she wore under it gaped. Deliberately she undid the last couple of buttons and pushed it aside.

Esteban's eyes flared. But he stood like a rock, his response under iron control.

Nicky took his hands and pulled gently. He resisted. She sank down on to the rug, urging him to join her. Esteban let her go but he did not follow her. He looked down at her broodingly.

'Last night you couldn't say you wanted me.' His voice was almost unrecognisable.

'I want you.'

Nicky lay back on the rug and stretched her arms behind her head. She did not care about her fire-lit nakedness. She lay there, eyes steady on his, offering herself without disguise.

Esteban knelt on one knee beside her. He caressed one lifting nipple as if he could not help himself. But he was watching her face.

'I'm possessive,' he said in a warning tone.

Nicky gave a little anticipatory shiver.

'So go ahead and possess me.'

It was said teasingly. But they both knew it was deadly serious. His eyes darkened.

'You don't have to pretend.'

'I want to make love with you,' Nicky said quietly. 'No pretending.' She was saying it to more than this man tonight. She was saying it to all the arid years when she had ached for Steve and not acknowledged it.

He gave a great sigh and came down on to the rug beside her.

'You'll get cold.'

'So warm me up.' Her own voice was unrecognisable too. Like the laughing provocation of the remark. Like the *confidence* of it.

He will think I do this sort of thing all the time, Nicky thought with just a flicker of concern.

But it was too late. Esteban flung himself out of the torn shirt. His other clothes followed, tossed away across the library like so many rags.

Esteban did not notice. His concentration was wholly on Nicky. He had said he was possessive; and he was. His hands swept down her body, claiming her, branding her. And his mouth was hungry.

Nicky was almost frightened for a second. She thought, *I didn't know*. And then her body took over.

She had never experienced such total absorption. Esteban explored without restraint and expected her to do the same. The only thing he seemed unaware of was how totally new this was to her.

Nicky's unpractised reflexes went into rapidly escalating response. A long way away, her mind watched and was amazed. But Nicky, shocked, scared and trusting, abandoned herself to Esteban.

It was like a tidal wave: not gradual but sudden, huge and terrifying. Nicky gasped and hung on to his shoulders. Esteban steadied her, murmuring. She was not sure what. Her ears were ringing as she was thrown up, up, up...

The momentum increased: his body's, hers. She felt tears and hardly noticed them as she strove fiercely.

Esteban flung back his head and shouted aloud. Suddenly Nicky convulsed. There was an explosion of light behind her eyes. She was *there*.

Afterwards they fell asleep from sheer exhaustion. But the cold meant their sleep was brief.

'I need to get you to bed,' said Esteban.

She hardly recognised him, his eyes were so warm. He

looked down at her with such rueful complicity and kissed one cold breast possessively.

'Or my next reason to keep you here will be hypothermia.'

He gathered her up, finding the old dressing gown and tucking it round her. This time she did not demand that he put her down. He carried her through the house to her room.

'What about you?' murmured Nicky, her head on his shoulder. She ran her hand down his naked spine, loving the feel of it. 'You must be freezing.'

'The exercise is keeping me warm,' he said drily as he mounted the stairs.

In her room he dropped her on to the bed and turned away.

'Don't go,' said Nicky, suddenly alarmed.

He grinned at her. 'No chance. But I've got something to wear in here somewhere. You don't want me freezing you to death.'

He pulled a towelling robe out of the wardrobe and slid his arms into it. Nicky watched for a moment. Her eyes assessed him with that new-found confidence.

She made up her mind. She snaked her way across the coverlet and began to pluck at the robe, teasing. Laughing, he pretended to fend her off. But she had learned her lesson well and the laughter did not last long for either of them. She stripped the robe away.

'We don't need that,' she said huskily.

They didn't.

It was not until early morning, when she lay wakeful with Esteban asleep beside her, that other thoughts returned to chill her blood. *What has happened to me?* Nicky thought.

She had gone wild. Felt wild. And now the wildness had burned itself out and left her on the other side of a great ravine, not quite sure how she had got there.

All her adult life men had accused her of coldness. Andrew Bolton had gone further when he'd called her a fraud. Nicky had accepted it. She had not even felt indignant. It was true. Now—

Suddenly she could not bear to lie there a moment longer.

She slid out of bed. And gasped. She had forgotten she was naked.

Behind her Esteban turned over, murmuring in protest. Nicky froze. But then he pulled the pillow under his chin and subsided again with a sigh.

The cold air struck at her shrinking skin. Nicky looked round for something to cover her. Then her feet tangled in his discarded robe. She remembered all too clearly how she had slid it off his shoulders. How she had twined round him, laughing, teasing, luring him… She shut her eyes at the memory.

Tell the truth, she told herself harshly. You were seducing him. Deliberately. You made all the running. Not once but twice. *You*. How could you?

Shivering, she bent and picked up the robe from where she had thrown it last night and huddled it round her. It smelled of his skin. Nicky held the lapel against her face and breathed Esteban in.

She sank on to the window seat. Outside the pre-dawn sky shimmered. Clouds rushed dizzyingly between the sea and the stars. Nicky felt as if she was falling. She braced herself against the cold stone of the window embrasure. It seemed as if her whole life was racing away out to sea with the clouds.

I'll never be the same, she thought.

Behind her, the man on the bed stirred. She sat very still. In vain. He moved again, more strongly. The bed creaked several times. Then stopped altogether.

Nicky did not turn her head but she heard him prop himself up on one elbow. She could feel him looking at her out of the darkness.

'What is it?' he said quietly.

Nicky did not know how to answer him. She knew she could not lie any longer. Some time during the night she has lost her ability to tell those light, necessary half truths with which she was used to defending herself from Andrew and men like him. Men who, ultimately, she had not cared about.

She shuddered at the implications of that. Did she care so much for Esteban Tremain, then?

But the truth—the whole truth—was so big and so complicated that she did not know where to start. Or whether Esteban would understand, even if she could find the words. She stared out at the turbulent sky, silenced by her own confusion.

Esteban slid out of bed and padded across to her.

'Nicky?'

He sounded almost tentative. Surely not. Not Esteban, the master of his life, his instincts and Hallam. And, now, of her body and her heart.

'Nicky, what is it?'

He cupped her shoulder. His palm was so warm that she felt the heat even through the material of his robe. Nicky shut her eyes.

She said, 'I'm not used—' And could not go on.

He waited. Her voice was clogged. She gave her head a little shake.

Esteban pulled at her shoulder gently, urging her to turn to him. Nicky resisted. She opened her eyes and stared out at the pre-dawn sky as if her life depended on it.

Eventually the pressure stopped. Esteban said gently, 'Used to what?'

It was a good question. Nicky could not answer it. She shook her head dumbly.

His hand began to move, almost absently, caressing her shoulder.

'Then let me guess.' His voice was warm. Amused, even. 'You're not used to four-poster beds? Medieval draughts? Making passionate love on top of a four-course meal?'

Nicky could not bear the tender, teasing note in his voice. She said harshly, 'I'm not used to sleeping with a man.'

The caressing hand stilled on her shoulder. There was a pause. It felt like the end of the world.

'Ah,' Esteban said at last.

She thought he would try to make her turn round again

but he did not. Staring out of the window, Nicky pulled his robe tighter round her. She was shivering. How could he stand there naked and not feel the cold? she thought with a flicker of temper.

He said as if he were no more than mildly interested, 'Is that supposed to mean that you usually sleep with a woman?'

Nicky gasped and swung round. '*No*. Of course not.'

In the dawn light she could see he was staring down at her gravely. His voice had misled her. He was not teasing at all. And he was a lot more than mildly interested. His eyes were passionately intent.

'How *can* you?' she choked.

There was a tiny pause.

'Well, at least it got you to look at me,' he pointed out drily.

'Oh, very clever.' Nicky was bitter. 'Are those the tactics you use in court?'

Esteban waved that aside as if it was not worth answering.

'The alternative is that you don't sleep with anyone,' he observed in a neutral voice. 'Are you trying to tell me you are a virgin?'

'After last night, don't you mean *were* a virgin?' Nicky flung back, suddenly and inexplicably furious.

This time the pause was charged. *Why did I say that?* Nicky thought. She held her breath. A part of her was utterly bewildered by what she was doing. Another part—the new, wild part—wanted to go on and on until she goaded him into... What?

'Yes,' said Esteban at last evenly. Too evenly. 'I'm glad you reminded me.'

He took hold of her, not gently at all, and hauled her to her feet. Nicky's head went back.

'Let me go,' she yelled. She was shaking with anger.

By contrast, Esteban was so quiet she could hardly hear him. 'Well?'

His naked body glimmered palely in the dark. Like some marble statue of a god, Nicky thought, crazily. You would

smash yourself to pieces if you fell against stone like that.
She rammed her forearm against his chest and levered herself
away. She was panting.

'What do you mean, "Well?"' she snarled.

'If you've got something to tell me, tell me.'

'Tell you? What would I have to tell you?'

His jaw was like stone, too.

He said with precision and absolutely no sign of emotion
at all, 'Is it true?' And when she did not answer he shook
her a little. 'Was I the first?'

He was not rough. He certainly did not hurt her. But Nicky
flinched as if from a blow. She was speechless.

Esteban said, 'That's it, isn't it? I was the first.' For a
moment Nicky stared at him as if he were speaking a foreign
language. Then, horribly, she began to laugh. He had been
the first to break down all her barriers. She laughed until she
was choking. Her breaths came in great gulps, straining her
ribs.

Esteban took his hands away. Nicky was laughing so hard,
she barely noticed. Esteban stepped away. She was alone.

Nicky put out a hand to the wall to steady herself. She
tried to control the crazy laughter but it spiralled up and up,
making her ears ring. She was light-headed with it.

And suddenly she was drenched in ice.

Nicky's eyes flew open in shock. Esteban was there again,
holding a nearly empty glass, and her face was wet. The
terrible laughter stopped dead. She put up a hand and rubbed
her eyes.

'Here. You'd better drink the rest.'

He handed her the glass. Nicky hesitated.

'It's only water,' he said briefly.

He must have brought the water from his own room. While
he was there he had taken the opportunity to pull on a shirt.
Clothed, he did not look like a marble god any more. He
looked a hundred times sexier.

Nicky took the tumbler from him and poured the water

down her throat as if it were medicine. She gave the mug back.

'Thank you,' she said in a small voice.

'You're welcome.'

It was bottled mineral water and he had brought it from his room. He poured some more and gave the glass back to her. This time she just sipped.

Esteban did not try to touch her. Instead he retreated to the end of the bed. He propped himself against one of the wooden barley sugar posts and crossed one tanned foot over the other.

'OK,' he said, as if they were working on some abstruse theorem to which there was a logical answer. 'What is it about sleeping with someone that you're not used to?'

Nicky folded her lips together.

'Is it because we don't know each other very well?'

'We don't know each other at all,' Nicky muttered.

'I wouldn't say that.' Suddenly, shockingly, there was a note of total intimacy in his voice. 'I know you cook like an angel. You don't like Renaissance painting. And you pack a mean screwdriver. It's a start.'

A start to what? Her own pulses told her.

'No,' said Nicky hoarsely. More to herself than to him.

Esteban folded his arms across his chest. He looked like a man who had suddenly scented an interesting debate and was willing to stick with it as long as it took.

'Are you going to tell me you're already in a steady relationship?' He sounded disbelieving.

Nicky winced. She had never managed a steady relationship. Never committed herself totally to anyone. How could he tell? Was it written all over her?

'You think what we've done involves some sort of betrayal?' he persisted.

The puzzled impatience was all too reminiscent of Steve on that moonlit beach.

'Only of myself,' Nicky said desolately.

Esteban snorted. 'You've taken a vow of celibacy?'

'You don't understand…'

'I understand all right.' Suddenly he was grim. 'We've got something between us. For a moment back there you woke up to it. Now the reaction has stopped fizzing and you're remembering that you don't like me. Well, tough. I don't like you all that much either. It doesn't make any difference.'

'Difference to what?' demanded Nicky. Though she knew.

Esteban looked at her across the shadowed room.

'The fact that we want each other,' he said quietly.

The room was cold. Outside the wind was rising. But Nicky's skin remembered the warmth of a Caribbean night and a scented breeze. She ought to tell him; she ought to tell him *now*. But something kept her tongue locked in a vice.

'Don't we?' said Esteban.

He held out a hand. Like a sleepwalker, Nicky went to him. The great bed towered over them like a ship. Nicky found she was shaking as if the world were breaking apart under her feet.

Esteban put his arms round her. The world steadied. But her heart didn't. Just like ten years ago.

She said, 'I have to tell you—'

'You're not used to it.' His voice was warm with amusement. 'I know.'

'Not that—before…'

But her words dwindled into suffocating silence. Esteban was too close, too intent. Her heart slammed as if it would drive itself out of her body and into his. She clung to him, shaking.

'Do you think I'm used to this?' Suddenly his voice was ragged. 'Do you think anyone could be?'

Nicky thought, He's shaking as much as I am.

She said harshly, 'Touch me.'

He got rid of the robe with agonising slowness. Bending, he moved his face across her throat, her shoulders, her breasts. He did not touch. He inhaled like a jungle animal scenting water—millimetres from her skin, but it burned like fire. He fell to one knee. Nicky grabbed his shirt to steady herself. She sobbed aloud.

It was exquisite. It was torture. It was the road to paradise she had glimpsed all those years ago under the Caribbean stars. It was *now*.

Esteban looked up. In the shadows she could not make out his expression. She did not need to. His ragged breathing, his low laugh said it all.

Pure triumph.

CHAPTER NINE

FOR the remainder of that night she did not dream. She awoke slowly. She was smiling and deliciously comfortable.

'Good morning,' said a voice. It sounded as if it was smiling too.

Nicky's eyes drifted open.

Four-poster. Open curtains to reveal a wide sky. The sea sparkling beyond a dark cliff. And dark eyes, warm with the knowledge of last night's lovemaking, so close they made her head swim.

Esteban!

She gave a little wriggle of pure pleasure. This morning he was wearing old jeans and an open-necked shirt. He had not shaved. His hair was still damp from the shower. Sheer lust took a firm grip of her abdomen. Nicky's smile widened. She held out her arms.

He kissed her but shook his head as she tried to pull him down to her.

'Time to get up. We have the fuzz calling on us this morning.'

Nicky laughed and let him go reluctantly. 'What time is it?'

'Nine.'

She yawned, stretching. The lifting breasts escaped the covers proudly. Esteban watched with amused appreciation.

'No use. It's time to get up. You can seduce me all you want when Mr Plod has gone.'

Nicky sent him a naughty look from under her lashes.

'Promise?'

He laughed. 'Behave yourself. How can I keep my mind on last night's intruder if you flourish those at me?'

He drew the covers firmly up to her chin. Nicky pulled a face.

'Spoilsport.'

He kissed her lingeringly. 'Temptress. There's coffee downstairs when you're ready.'

He went clattering down the hallway, whistling. Nicky sat up and considered what to wear. Last night's clothes were hopelessly creased. She compromised on her working trousers and a clean shirt of Esteban's which she filched from his drawer. It was not, after all, the first time she had worn a shirt of his.

The thought stopped her dead in her tracks. Her radiance dimmed. *I've got to tell him,* she thought. Now more than ever he had the right to know. She did not look forward to it.

So it was a constrained Nicky who went into the kitchen ten minutes later. Esteban was not constrained at all. He was slicing bread for a toaster which now worked. He was not actually singing, Nicky allowed, but he looked as if he might break into song at any moment.

She set her teeth.

'Esteban—there's something—'

He waved the bread knife in greeting.

'Feeling ready to face the law now you've got your clothes on?'

I will not blush, Nicky thought, indignant at this lack of sensitivity. I will not.

'I'm fine,' she said repressively.

Esteban looked her up and down appreciatively. 'You are indeed.'

For the first time that she could remember under a look like that, Nicky found she had no desire to clamp her arms across her breasts. No urge to hide. She liked Esteban looking at her. She was glad that he seemed to like what he saw. She forgot about telling him anything that he did not already know and gave a low, delighted laugh. She was not going to feel outclassed by his stepfather's Renaissance nymphs ever again.

He held out an arm. She went and leaned against him. He kissed her hair absently and carried on cooking one-handed.

'Toast? Cereal? The full English breakfast?'

Nicky rubbed her face against his shoulder. 'Who needs food?'

'That's what I like to hear. An appreciative woman.'

He slipped bread into the toaster and poured her coffee. Nicky took it and added milk.

'I took one of your shirts.'

Esteban's eyes laughed down at her. 'I noticed. I look forward to taking it back.'

Nicky purred. His arm tightened. But there was a sharp ring from the front-door bell.

'Just as well,' said Esteban ruefully. 'Or Mr Plod could have been seriously embarrassed.'

He went to let in the policeman.

There was only one and he had clearly known Esteban for years. He accepted coffee and toast and sat down at the kitchen table.

'Well, what can you tell me about your intruder?' he said, pulling out a grubby notebook.

Esteban gave him a concise account. The policeman wrote it down painstakingly. He looked at Nicky for corroboration.

'I didn't see anyone,' Nicky said apologetically.

'That's a pity. Still, at least he didn't come back after you'd called us. They do sometimes, you know. The cheek of these villains.'

Nicky thought of what the intruder would have found if he had returned to the library. She looked towards Esteban, her expression stunned. He kept a poker face but his eyes were dancing.

'Just as well he didn't,' he agreed gravely.

'Better show me where he got in, then,' said the policeman, getting up.

Esteban came back ten minutes later.

'They're bringing up a team to dust for fingerprints. I said we'd get out and leave them to it.'

'Very wise,' said Nicky drily.

He rubbed the back of her neck as if he had been doing it all his life.

'That's what I thought. God knows how long I'd be able to keep my hands off you. The wind has dropped. Come on.'

He insisted on lending her heavy boots as well as the waxed jacket. Nicky let him lace the boots up for her. She felt more cared for than she ever had in her life. She almost said so. But their unconfessed history kept her silent.

The path he chose wound downhill away from the sea. The pale sun, only just above the horizon, illuminated a sky like a powdered rainbow—the colours of amethyst, black cherry, toast. Sharp black shadows of trees lay across a lawn frosted to white. The air had the sharp tang of cold champagne.

Nicky drew a long breath.

'It is beautiful.'

Esteban looked down at her. 'I think so,' he said quietly. 'That's partly why I have tried to keep it going. Not just for my stepfather, though of course he loves it. If he thought he could never come back here, he would give up, I think.'

Nicky was startled. 'And is that a possibility?'

'Not as long as I can earn enough to pay the next bill,' Esteban said grimly.

'And can you?'

'Over time, yes. But we have our hairy moments.'

There was something in his voice which made Nicky scan his expression alertly.

'And is now one of those?'

Esteban was silent for a moment. Then he said slowly, 'Do you know me so well? Already?'

For some reason it made Nicky uncomfortable.

'I just thought—'

'Rightly.'

He strode on for a while in silence.

Then he said in a level tone, 'Now is indeed one of those moments. My stepfather's convalescent home has cost a fortune; between that and a poor summer, the deficit has got out of hand. The farm is up to the limit on its overdraft. I've got a big job in New Zealand next week which will pay the bills eventually. But clients can take their time to pay up.'

'Don't I know it,' said Nicky with feeling.

Esteban nodded. 'So meanwhile I'm scrabbling round to keep us afloat. Yesterday I talked Patrick into selling one of the paintings at last. But that could take almost as long to bring money in as my New Zealand clients.' He laughed, half angry half resigned. 'Impasse. I can't think of a solution.'

But Nicky was sensitised to his moods now. 'What's the solution you don't want to think about?'

Esteban jumped. 'Are you reading my mind?' He looked down at her searchingly.

There was a pause. He had not been able to find gloves for her to borrow. Now he took her naked hand and held it as they walked. Nicky's cold fingers twitched, then twined with his. Oh, *last night*. He had not answered her question but suddenly she did not care.

His hand tightened, hard. She knew he was thinking of last night too. It was sobering, this silent communication.

Esteban said slowly, 'It feels like we've always been lovers. You seem to know me so well. But—'

Nicky's hand tensed in his.

'Why do I think there's something you're not telling me?'

It was the perfect opportunity. She knew she had to do it. But somehow, when it came to it, she could not. *Later*, she promised herself.

She removed her hand from his and started to ask about the countryside. Esteban let her. But his expression promised that the subject was not closed.

From the smooth sweep of sward they plunged into an overgrown path. Puffball heads of dead flowers drifted against their clothes like frosted feathers.

'What are these?'

'Old man's beard,' Esteban told her. He removed one from her shoulder and held it out for her to see. 'A wild clematis. A weed.'

'It's beautiful,' said Nicky, watching it blow away down the path ahead of them.

'You will get on with Patrick. He likes weeds too.' He paused, then added deliberately, 'To say nothing of girls who look like his favourite nymphs.'

Nicky blushed but said honestly, 'Now you're reading *my* mind. Oh, not that I look like them. But I thought this morning that I sort of understood how they felt.' She looked up at him. 'I've never felt that before. Can you understand?'

Esteban's face was serious. He took her hand again. 'I think you and I have a lot of talking to do.'

They walked on, silent in their total intimacy.

The path dipped steeply into a wood. Nicky heard a rush of water. Then she saw the stream. It was below them, splashing busily as it eddied round smooth rocks and swirled about the struts of a rickety wooden bridge. She stopped and drew a long, delighted breath.

Across the stream the steep bank was vivid green all the way from the top to a line roughly opposite to where they were standing. Then it turned abruptly silver where the sun had not yet reached the frozen dew. It was very cold.

Nicky stood utterly still. She was conscious of Esteban behind her, the warmth of his body, his breath in her hair. His arms went round her waist. She tipped her head back, feeling his strength as she leaned against him, looking.

She said softly, 'It's magic.'

His arms tightened. But his voice was teasing when he answered, 'And you said you didn't do magic.'

For a moment she was bewildered. Then she remembered shouting at him in the showroom just a few days ago. It felt like another dimension of time.

'The magic seems to be mutual.'

'Yes.' But he was no longer teasing. 'Nicky—'

'Yes?'

He looked down at their locked hands. 'This is—unexpected. I can't help thinking I've bounced you into something you weren't prepared for.'

Nicky was shaken to the heart. After a moment she said evasively, 'Not that unexpected. You said you wanted more than a truce, after all.'

'Yes, I did, didn't I?' He looked up. 'I didn't realise how much more. So—it matters that you're holding out on me.'

Nicky looked away. He turned her cold face back towards him.

'How about telling me the truth now?' he said gently.

She thought, *Tell him now.* She even opened her mouth to frame the words.

'Whatever it is, I can deal with it,' he promised. 'Just tell me.'

Nicky looked in his eyes and read all the possessive intensity he had warned her about. Oh, yes, he could deal with anything, she thought. The problem was, could she? If she told him and Esteban saw her once again as the sexy, callow schoolgirl he had fought off, she thought she would die of shame.

She could not do it. He gave a small sigh.

'OK. Leave it for the moment.' He looked down at their hands again. 'You're frozen. Let's get you warmed up. Then we'll talk.'

He set a brisk pace until they came to the outskirts of a village. In the distance she recognised the inn where they had eaten last night.

'We must have walked miles,' Nicky said, glad of a neutral subject.

'A few. But we've walked straight down the hillside. The road winds. Tired?'

'Just beginning to flag.'

'Step out, then. Ian will have a fire in the snug and I have no doubt he will rustle us up a ploughman's lunch if we ask for it.'

Nicky's stomach rumbled. She clutched it, laughing.

'After last night's meal I thought I'd never want to eat again. But I was wrong.'

'You've had a lot of exercise since then.' Esteban's tone was bland.

Nicky looked at him sharply. His face was perfectly serious. So why did she think he was laughing? No, *know* he was laughing. She thought, Because I'm in love with him.

She stopped dead. Esteban looked down at her, startled. 'Stitch?'

Nicky felt as if she had walked into a brick wall. She shook her head to clear it. 'Yes. No. Not really.'

I'm in love with him. *I'm in love with him.* I've always been in love with him. Why didn't I realise it?

That was why she had thought about him, dreamed about him. That was why his image had haunted her all her adult life, interposing itself between her and any other man. It was not that his rejection had hurt so much that she did not dare to trust anyone ever again. It was that she was still in love with the man on the moonlit beach.

Only now he was called Esteban Tremain. And when he looked at her he did not despise her any more. He liked her; he laughed at her; he certainly wanted her.

But did he love her? Nicky's heart fluttered uneasily. She could read his moods but she could not read that. She realised she had not the slightest idea.

He touches me as if he loves me, thought Nicky, walking on in silence. Surely he loves me. It feels as if he does, said her hopeful heart.

Well, it would, wouldn't it? said her brain. After all, what do you know about love? You've been in the deep freeze for ten years. It hasn't exactly given you a wealth of experience to draw on. Whereas if there's one thing Esteban Tremain has by the bucketful it's experience. And he didn't say a word about love.

And you haven't said a word about your moonlit beach, her heart reminded her. Trust is a two-way thing, you know.

Nicky bit her lip.

'Esteban—' she began.

But they had reached the pub. He held the door for her.

'Go and get warm by the fire,' he urged gently. 'The snug is through there. I'll bring the drinks. What do you want?'

'Oh, anything,' said Nicky distractedly.

She went where he pointed. Her brain was in a whirl.

Which must have been why she hardly noticed the man standing in the lee of the staircase in the small telephone booth. Deep in thought, she walked past him, oblivious.

It was he who, looking up, nearly dropped the phone. He flung it back on its cradle and dashed out of the booth.

'Nick? It *is* you. Nicky.'

She turned then.

'Ben.' She stared, not believing it. 'What on earth are you doing here?'

Her brother was looking shocked. 'I was going to ask the same thing. Oh, Lord.'

He sounded guilty, Nicky realised. He looked quickly over his shoulder. Then he took her by the shoulder and almost pushed her out of the hallway into the empty snug.

'Have you come looking for me?' he demanded in a low, urgent voice.

Nicky thought she had never seen her laid-back brother so agitated.

'I'm working,' she said in bewilderment. 'I told you when we had lunch. The kitchen where everything had gone wrong. The house is up the cliff. We've just walked in.'

Ben looked at her with horror. 'You mean Hallam Hall?'

'Yes,' said Nicky, puzzled.

'For Tremain?' He sounded appalled.

'Yes. What's wrong?'

'I told you the man was bad news,' said Ben intensely. 'I *told* you not to have anything to do with him.'

Nicky began to feel alarmed.

'What do you mean? How do you know Esteban?'

Ben brushed that aside. 'You've got to get out. Go back to London now.'

An unwelcome suspicion crept over Nicky. She drew a steadying breath and said again, 'What are you doing here, Ben?'

'It's a job,' he muttered. 'Just a job.'

Nicky knew her freewheeling brother. 'What sort of job?' she said with foreboding.

'A girl I know,' he said in a rapid undertone. 'Tremain dropped her flat when he'd had what he wanted. She'd give up everything for him. She put me on a retainer to watch him and—well, she just wanted him to hurt a bit.'

'Hurt…?' Nicky was speechless.

'Nothing dangerous,' Ben said hastily. 'I told her I didn't do things like that. Just a bit of damage. Preferably with high repair bills,' he added in a practical tone.

She thought, This is my brother and I don't know him at all. Ben saw her expression. He shifted uncomfortably.

'It was cash in hand,' he muttered. 'I couldn't keep coming to you. Anyway—' his confidence reasserted itself '—he deserved it.'

'Deserved what?' said Nicky. Though she was almost sure she knew.

That was clearly what Ben thought. He said impatiently, 'I—er—adjusted the kitchen appliances. And his car.'

Ben had to be the intruder. The irony of it hit her. Nicky gave a harsh laugh.

Ben took an urgent step forward. 'Nick—'

'*My* car,' she told him.

'What?'

'You're not very good at this, are you, Ben? Did you really think Esteban would drive an urban runabout? That's mine.'

Ben whitened. 'I don't believe it.'

'He has a Jaguar XJ8. I imagine it was garaged in the old stables when you were snooping around.'

'I can't have been that stupid. I *can't*.'

Nicky shrugged. 'So the one with the massive repair bill is me.'

Ben looked round wildly as if he was trying to find another explanation.

'And I've been making a statement to the police this morning,' she said, her voice shaking. 'About the intruder last night.'

Ben winced.

'What am I going to do?' she said, more to herself than to him. 'How am I going to tell Esteban?'

'Tell me what?' said Esteban, coming into the snug with a couple of tankards.

Nicky looked round. She did not say anything. Her face said it for her.

Esteban's eyebrows flew up. 'What—?'

And then he saw Ben. He stopped dead. Ben took hold of her elbow. Nicky was wretched. 'This is—'

Esteban was not listening to her. She saw that he recognised Ben. The hostility was instant and unequivocal.

'We haven't been introduced,' he said with barbed courtesy. 'But didn't we nearly meet a few days ago?'

Ben said, 'You're Esteban Tremain.'

Esteban was being civilised. He put the drinks down and gave Ben a wide, polite smile. 'And you're Nicola's private life.'

'*No,*' said Nicky instinctively.

Ben's grip on her elbow tightened painfully and held her silent.

'You could say that,' he drawled.

Esteban was not that civilised. For a brief second his eyes flashed molten with rage. 'And I think,' he said with dangerous quietness, 'that you're my intruder of last night.'

Ben gave a mocking laugh. Nicky wrenched her elbow out of his grip.

'That's enough,' she said harshly. 'There have been enough lies. No more.'

'Lies?' said Esteban very quietly.

Ben said, 'Nicky—'

They both ignored him.

'So this was what you weren't telling me.'

Nicky met Esteban's eyes. She thought she had never seen such passion; such pain; such distaste. A cold hand clutched at her heart.

'I can explain…'

'I'm sure you can.'

He was very gentle and remote as the moon. If it had not been for those bitter eyes, she would have thought he did not care a snap of his fingers, one way or the other.

'As a liar, you're inspired,' he told her in congratulatory tones.

'Take that back,' said Ben fiercely.

Nicky turned on him. 'Go away. You've done enough harm.'

Ben paled. 'I never meant—'

'Just go.'

He did. The door of the snug banged behind him.

In the sudden silence, Esteban said, 'Were the lies really necessary?'

Nicky tried to marshal her thoughts. It was not easy with him standing there looking as if he hated her. She swallowed.

'I should have told you,' she said, not very coherently.

His face was a mask. 'I asked you if there was anyone else. I asked you.'

She sensed a slow fury building behind the mask. She refused to let herself be intimidated but it was an effort. She shook her head and said quietly, 'Not that. It's me.'

Esteban said nothing. His concentration was total.

Nicky moistened her lips. 'You and I— You've forgotten— We met before,' she finished baldly.

Esteban looked arrested. His brows twitched together in a black frown. But he still said nothing.

'I know you don't remember. Well, it wasn't very important. Except it was to me,' Nicky said, stumbling over the words as if she were a teenager again.

'What are you talking about?' It ripped out, savage.

Nicky quailed. But she had to tell him the whole truth now. Even if he looked at her with contempt or loathing afterwards, she could not let him go on thinking she had conspired with Ben against him.

'Ten years ago,' she said rapidly. 'Cotton Island. I worked on your boat one night—'

An oath, shocking in its ferocity, cut her short. Nicky flinched as if from a blow. Esteban's face was not a mask any more. He looked as if he was going to burst into flames of rage.

'*Pompilia.*' He spat it out like a snake striking.

Nicky stood fast but it was an effort. 'Th—that was my father's boat.'

A muscle worked in his cheek. 'Which he sold on May 4th that year.'

Nicky stared. 'What?'

'All I knew about you was that you were nearly sixteen and lived on *Pompilia*,' he said evenly. 'I traced that bloody boat all round the world. Do you know how many times she has been sold?'

'N-no.'

'I do. And I know the name of everyone who ever owned her or chartered her. There's no Piper on the list.'

Nicky could not believe Esteban had done that. She said blankly, 'Leon always sets up a company to own his boats. He says it's better for the insurance or something.'

'So why didn't he record himself as a shareholder of the company? He wasn't on *any* of the lists, believe me.'

'Trying to keep one step ahead of the creditors, I should think,' Nicky was shaken into admitting.

Esteban swore again.

'I suppose that's why he never seems to have moored at any decent harbour? Never shown his papers anywhere in the Caribbean? Never listed crew and passengers when he put to sea?'

Nicky stared. 'Are you supposed to?'

'It's a good idea,' said Esteban with restraint, 'if the boat gets into trouble, that the rescue services know how many people they're looking for.'

'Oh.'

'He was completely irresponsible, wasn't he?' Esteban was icy with fury. 'My investigators could not find any trace of *Pompilia* until, I suppose, he sold her.'

'Investigators!' Nicky was alarmed. 'Why did you try to find him?'

'I didn't. I tried to find you.'

She stared, astonished into blank silence.

He said more calmly, 'I wasn't proud of myself. You were so young. I should have kept a lid on the situation. When I had time to think about it, I realised—' He broke off. 'But you'd gone. That damned boat had disappeared. None of the port authorities seemed to know anything about it. Even the good old boys in the yacht clubs hadn't got any worthwhile gossip. I didn't know where to start looking.' He gave a sharp sigh. 'I didn't even know whether I ought to.'

Nicky swallowed. 'Why?' she said in a small voice.

'My motives are best described as mixed.' He looked at her broodingly.

She said, 'I thought you despised me. My whole life I've thought you despised me.'

His mouth twisted. 'Was that what this was all about?'

Nicky did not know what he was talking about. 'All what?'

He gestured at the door through which Ben had departed.

'The elaborate set-up.'

'The *what*?'

'Ben,' he said with distaste. 'Isn't that his name? It was a plot, wasn't it?'

Nicky winced. She hated having to admit what Ben had done.

'Yes,' she said in a low, shamed voice.

Esteban looked like stone.

'I should have guessed it,' he said harshly. 'If something is too good to be true, it means it isn't true.'

Nicky did not understand. So she said nothing. He gave a hard laugh.

'You even warned me, didn't you? I should have listened to you more carefully.'

He sounded so angry. This was a nightmare.

'Warned you?'

'"I don't like being messed about,"' he quoted savagely. 'Is that what you think I did, all those years ago? Messed you about?'

Something inside Nicky wanted to reach out to him; almost, if it had not been ridiculous, to comfort him. He stared at her as if he had never seen a specimen like her. As if she filled him with loathing. Nicky flinched.

'I thought I knew you. I didn't, did I? Not for a second. Every word, every gesture—it was all planned. And all false.'

'No,' said Nicky, understanding at last.

It was too late.

Esteban took a hasty step towards her. Nicky stared as if she had never seen him before. His mouth was compressed into a line of rigid control but the dark eyes were molten.

'You wanted your revenge, didn't you? Well, you had it.'

He seized her shoulders. Nicky was too dazed even to resist.

'And now I'll take mine.'

She read violent pain in his eyes. She put up a wavering hand, half protest, half caress. He caught it and held her immobile. His mouth came down on hers.

It was an assault on her deepest feelings. It felt as if he wanted to drain all the passion from her to the dregs. As if, when he had finished with her, she would be a bloodless ghost. He did not use his physical strength against her; he used furious desire. Mutual desire.

When he let her go, Nicky felt naked and broken. Her legs buckled. She had to grab hold of a chair-back to keep her upright.

Esteban looked at her as if he hated her. As if she had made him hate himself.

'You win.' It was so low she could hardly hear him.

He turned his back with an awful finality. And walked out.

CHAPTER TEN

BEN offered to take her back to London. He was very chastened. Nicky refused.

'If you want to do anything for me, you can get my bag back from Hallam Hall,' she said.

Ben looked appalled. 'Tremain will kill me.'

Nicky was too weary to care. She shrugged.

'What has the guy done to you?' said Ben, torn between alarm and affront. He was not used to such treatment from his sister.

'Not him. Me. I did it all,' said Nicky.

'You're not yourself.'

Her laugh broke in the middle.

Ben doesn't know me, she thought. Esteban doesn't know me. I don't even know myself any more.

She turned away. She had never felt so lonely in her life.

She travelled back to London on the train, thanking heaven for credit cards and the forethought which had made her tuck her wallet into the back pocket of her jeans. She did not have her clothes, her make-up or her toothbrush but she had her keys and the means to get some money. The rest, if Ben did not retrieve her bag, was expendable.

She collected bread and milk and a couple of escapist videos and spent the weekend trying to put Esteban Tremain out of her mind. It was not a success.

What has happened to me? Nicky thought.

For years she had hated the man she knew as Steve. In London, before she'd known who he was, she had recognised Esteban as a male predator instinctively. It had sent her into full retreat from him. And then at Hallam Hall everything had changed. Why?

Was it that first evening? She had not been very happy about spending the night alone in the castle. No, she thought in disgust, you can't get out of it that way. If that was the reason you would have fallen into bed with him the first night. You didn't.

The television screen flickered unnoticed. Nicky pressed the back of her fist to her mouth to stop herself crying out. Her lips was still tender from that final, forceful kiss. It was a potent reminder of the passion that had shaken her to the core. Not just Esteban's passion, either. Even as she realised that he would never forgive her, she recognised the depth of her need of him.

It was not just desire, thought Nicky. Heaven knew, her physical response to Esteban had left her with a hollow craving she did not think would ever be assuaged. But what haunted her was the hurt she had seen in his eyes behind the anger and betrayal.

If only she had never got involved with him again. Why on earth had she done it? Nicky demanded of herself. Because she had, hadn't she? Esteban might have been furious because of a misunderstanding. But he would not have had the chance to misunderstand, if she had not allowed him to make love to her.

Allowed him! Nicky stared sightless at the television screen. Who was she kidding? She had responded to him right from the start. But when she had failed to tell him she wanted him he had stopped and gone away at once. In the end, it was she who had initiated making love. It was all her own doing. Her responsibility. She could hardly say he'd seduced her, could she?

Not that it would be any better if you could, Nicky told herself in disgust. Which would you rather be—a weak-minded wimp who can't say no to an attractive man? Or a vamp who made all the running?

Neither, Nicky thought passionately. I want to be myself

again. No weaknesses, no commitments and nothing to be ashamed of either. In full control of my life at all times. I want that night when we drove each other wild never to have happened.

She curled up into a tight ball of misery on the sofa. She sat through three videos, none of which she could remember a word of. In the end sheer physical exhaustion released her. She slept.

On Monday she went to work as usual, except that she carried with her a large package. The first thing she had done when she'd got back to her flat was parcel up the boots and jacket he had lent her together with the shirt she had purloined. Her eyes filled, looking at the shirt, remembering how he had said he looked forward to taking it off. How it had made her shiver with anticipation.

She gave the package to Sally.

'Ship it to Hallam Hall,' she said crisply.

Sally took one look at her face and decided to ask no questions.

The others tiptoed respectfully round Nicky for the rest of the week. And Nicky, working like an automaton, got through a phenomenal amount of work, looked as if she was made of wood and never mentioned Esteban Tremain at all. Not even when a courier brought her suitcase and the showroom resonated with tactful silence.

Once Caroline wondered aloud whether he would be coming in to pay his bill.

'He's in New Zealand,' said Nicky, not looking up from her work. 'He won't pay the bill for weeks.'

The cheque came the next day. There was no letter with it. Martin thanked heaven. Nicky's expression became more wooden than ever.

Esteban was working all hours in final preparation for his trip. He was not best pleased when a tall, handsome man presented himself in the doorway of his room. He did not, however, as a hovering clerk half expected, throw him out.

'Felipe,' he said coldly.

He stood up, pulling on his jacket, and went forward to shake hands formally. The man who came in was sublimely confident, from his expensive tailoring to the grey wings of discreetly styled hair. He looked distinguished, like an ambassador, Esteban thought dispassionately. Or a film star who played a lot of ambassadors.

'You're busy,' the man said with easy charm. 'Forgive me. But I'm not in London for long this time.'

Esteban shrugged and closed the door behind him.

Felipe's smile was a brilliant flash of white in a tanned face. The likeness was unmistakable. They had the same high-bridged nose, the same deep eyes. Esteban knew it. It gave him no pleasure.

'I won't keep you from your work long. I wanted to see you.'

Esteban received the information without enthusiasm. 'Evidently. Why?'

The tall man sighed. 'Don't you think this feud has gone on long enough?'

Esteban did not answer that. 'What do you want?'

'I heard you were having some problems,' the other man said carefully. 'I wanted you to know that I am here.'

Esteban looked at him for a long moment, his eyes hard. 'I don't think Patrick would be happy to take your money,' he said at last, evenly.

'And you? What do you feel?'

Esteban just looked at him.

There was a sharp silence. Then the man nodded, as if that was what he expected.

'I see. I'm sorry. I hoped that after all this time you could understand, even if you could not forgive.'

Esteban made an abrupt movement, dismissing it.

'I'm not your judge, Felipe. It's not up to me.'

'In your place, I don't suppose I would forgive either,' the man said ruefully. 'In some ways we are so alike.'

Esteban did not answer that but he stiffened noticeably.

The man hesitated, inspecting a portrait of a grim-faced judge in full robes. Then, as if he was making a last gamble, he swung round to face Esteban.

'Esteban—your mother and I were too young. She hated being so far from her family and I resented not being enough for her. I never meant to hurt her,' he said with desperate earnestness. 'Surely you can understand now, even if you couldn't when you were ten. I just didn't seem to be able to control myself. And she—'

'Oh, yes,' said Esteban, as if he could not bear to hear any more. 'I can understand that. More than I ever wanted to.'

Felipe stopped dead. 'What?'

'The genes run true,' Esteban said curtly.

'*What?*'

'That's why I'm the last person to sit in judgement on you.'

He started to gather up the papers on his desk. Felipe watched him.

'What is this?'

Esteban's jaw set. He was clearly regretting his outburst. He did not look up.

Felipe said slowly, 'It's not just me you have to forgive, is it?'

Esteban's hands stilled. He looked up at last. His eyes were agonised.

He burst out as if he could no longer contain himself, 'Oh, God, Father. I hurt her. I must have been mad. I don't know what to *do*.'

Nicky's bruises faded but her inhuman efficiency did not. Her colleagues watched with increasing concern. When Ben rang to speak to her on Friday morning, Martin de Vries intercepted the call and closed the door to his office firmly.

'What's wrong with her?' he demanded. 'I've never seen her like this.'

'Neither have I,' said Ben miserably. 'She won't speak to

me when I call her at work. And at home she keeps the answering machine on and won't answer the door.'

'Bad,' said Martin. 'Do you know why?'

Ben admitted it.

'Then you'd better come round here and talk to her. I'll make sure she stays late tonight.'

He did. When she saw Ben, Nicky gave the first sign of life he had seen in a week.

'Get out of here,' she cried.

But Ben had toughened up during a wretched week. He seized her by the arms and held her still.

'Listen to me, Nick,' he said urgently. 'I've talked to the police. They say Tremain may withdraw the complaint.'

Nicky's face lost all colour. She stopped struggling in his grasp. Her eyes fixed on him painfully.

Ben drew a long breath. 'He won't talk to me. Can you try? Please?'

Nicky flinched. 'He's out of the country.'

'No, he isn't,' Ben said eagerly. 'He's at his chambers. I've just come from there.'

She hesitated. 'He hasn't tried to get in touch with me. How can I—?'

But Ben was a much loved brother, she reasoned. They had always got each other out of scrapes. And she had spent some considerable time alone with Esteban Tremain, after all. Another twenty minutes wouldn't hurt. Or wouldn't hurt any more than she hurt already.

'Oh, all right,' she said.

People worked late in chambers every night but Friday. That was the day of the week that they cleared their desks at four, or earlier, packed children or the tools of seduction into their cars, and piled off for the weekend in the country. Esteban had heard them clattering downstairs into the dark evening as the building emptied.

Anne appeared in the doorway.

'The courier has collected the papers for Auckland. I've

typed the Vereker Opinion but I'm only halfway through
Raleigh Processors.'

Esteban blinked. His eyes were gritty with tiredness.

'That's OK. As long as I can have it by Monday afternoon.
Anything else?'

Anne hesitated. 'Well—there's a woman. She didn't say
what she wanted but she kept talking about the police. She's
in the clerks' room.'

Esteban was puzzled. 'Police?'

'Could be blackmail,' said Anne, who had seen a lot of
life since she'd started working for a barrister. 'Won't give
her name. Blonde and gorgeous.'

'Blonde?'

Esteban was on his feet and out of the door before Anne
could answer. No waistcoat, no jacket, and his shirt-sleeves
rolled up to reveal muscular forearms. He did not seem to
notice, much less care. He positively ran down the corridor.
The clerks, thought Anne, would have the shock of their lives
if they saw him now.

But the clerks' room was empty except for a slim blonde
figure huddled in a damp coat.

Nicky had paced up and down in the courtyard for a long
time before she'd plucked up the courage to go in. As she
looked up at Esteban's tempestuous entrance, her heart nearly
failed her. He looked so wild. So—her mouth dried—utterly
sexy.

'It is you,' he said in an odd tone.

She could not think of a thing to say.

He pushed a hand through his hair. She had never seen
him so dishevelled. She wanted to smooth it so badly it was
like a physical need. She thrust her hands up her sleeves and
folded her lips together, speechless.

'What are you doing here?'

'I—' Her heart was beating so hard she thought he must
be able to hear it.

'Come to my room,' he said harshly.

Her pulses leaped. She followed him without a word.

'Now,' he said, closing the door firmly and putting his back to it as if he would never let her out again, 'you're here. Why?'

Nicky tried to remember. The look in his eyes did not make it easy. 'M-my brother.'

'Who?' He looked impatient.

'He said you would withdraw the charges if I came to see you,' she said rapidly.

He looked stunned. 'That man was your *brother*?'

Nicky nodded. 'He was stupid,' she said rapidly. 'But if you hadn't treated that woman Francesca so badly, she would never have convinced him to help in the first place. He's never done anything like that before. And he really—'

Esteban breathed hard. 'Nicky—'

'—doesn't know how he could be so stupid. What?'

'Shut up,' said Esteban, coming firmly towards her and taking her in his arms. 'Shut up. Shut up. *Shut up.*'

He threw a key on to the desk and kissed her comprehensively. Nicky gave a small sob.

'You can't want me. Not after the way I lied.'

'You didn't lie,' said Esteban, kissing her throat, her chin, her eyelids. He sounded breathless. 'You just forgot to tell me all the truth. And you would be surprised what I can want.'

Not lifting his mouth from her skin, he pushed the coat off her shoulders. Her business suit followed. His hands were practised but not quite steady.

'Oh, God, Nicky, I thought I'd lost you. I've got to have you *now*.'

They sank on to the floor.

It was a long time later when Nicky stirred in his arms and said dreamily, 'I think we both just behaved appallingly.' She sounded rather proud of herself.

Esteban was shaken by a soundless laugh. He hugged her close. 'Somebody ought to paint it,' he agreed lazily.

'Completely out of control.' Nicky was warming to her theme.

He kissed her. 'Don't wind me up, you baggage. I've never had any control where you're concerned.' He paused, then said painfully, 'That was what scared me so much in the Caribbean.'

Nicky struggled up on one elbow and stared down at him, astonished.

'Scared? You?'

He reached up a wondering hand and traced her mouth.

'I'd seen my father go crazy. I thought I was different. It took just one car ride and being hit on the foot with a jar of coffee to show me I was exactly the same. And you were fifteen, for God's sake.'

Nicky said incredulously, 'You *do* remember.'

He sat up. 'I remember all right.'

She gave a shiver, half voluptuous, half sad.

He said with difficulty, 'I don't know how I didn't recognise you.'

Nicky said wisely, 'You probably didn't want to. I didn't. I'm pretty certain I knew before I knew I knew, if you follow me.'

Esteban looked sober. 'When did you know for sure?'

'When I saw a photograph in your room. You were wearing sunglasses. It just—clicked into place. I didn't know what to do.'

'Why on earth didn't you tell me?' He sounded as if he was suffering.

Nicky shook her head. 'At first I just wanted to run. Later—' She bent her head, blushing. 'I meant to. But things kept interrupting. And then I lost my nerve.'

Esteban's arm clamped her to him. 'Were you so scared of me?'

Nicky looked at him in surprise. He looked sick.

It gave her courage to say, 'Not scared exactly. But I've always been sort of ashamed.'

'*Ashamed?* Of what, for heaven's sake?'

Nicky looked down at her rosy nakedness. She was reclining against Esteban's shoulder for all the world like one of Hallam's more disreputable nymphs. She smiled.

'It may be difficult to believe just at this moment, but I used to hate men looking at me.'

He did not smile back. His arm tightened painfully and she felt his lips move in her hair.

'Piers and his friends did quite a number on you, didn't they?'

'Not the number that you did. You were the one who called me a voluptuous Cleopatra.' Her smile died. 'You were the one who didn't want me.'

'I wanted you.'

She looked up. 'But—'

'You say you were ashamed. What do you think I was?' His voice was harsh. 'You were so young and scared and I—lost control. I was worse than Felipe.'

'*No,*' said Nicky, dazed.

'And then it happened all over again last week. Like a recurring nightmare. When I thought you'd set me up I went mad for a moment. I almost hated you. I wanted to hurt you.'

Nicky flinched. But she said steadily, 'But you didn't.'

He drew away a little and lifted her chin so she had to look up at him. He touched her mouth gently. His face twisted. 'You're very generous. I know I wasn't—kind.'

Nicky's eyes were steady. 'No. But I probably deserved it.'

'Don't say that,' he said sharply. 'It makes me feel like Felipe.' He shut his eyes for a moment. 'I always dreaded—' Nicky hugged him. 'You were shocked and you nearly lost it for a moment. That's all. You didn't *hurt* me. Not the way you hurt yourself.'

He said on a little shaken breath, 'Oh, Nicky, I love you. I'll never hurt you again. I swear it.'

He held her very tightly.

Nicky said, 'So why have you let this whole week pass without a word? Why did you just send that beastly suitcase back to the showroom? It seemed like you didn't want me again.'

He lifted his head and looked down at her eloquently.

'Is that what it seems like?' he asked drily.

Nicky gave a little wriggle of pleasure.

'Well, maybe not just at this moment,' she allowed. 'But it was pretty horrible marching about outside trying to get up my courage. It was raining too.' She shivered.

'You're cold,' said Esteban remorsefully.

He looked round for her clothes. They were strewn widely and he could not find her tights. But he collected the rest and helped her to dress, kissing her as he helped her pull on the garments.

'Well, you don't look very respectable, my darling,' he said, sweeping her hair clear of her collar and kissing her ear, 'but at least you won't die of cold before I get you home.'

Nicky was suddenly shy.

'Home?'

'My home,' Esteban said firmly. 'I'm not letting you out of my sight again until you marry me. I have an apartment below Tower Bridge.'

Nicky raised her eyebrows. 'And what about my apartment?'

Esteban was not thrown. 'Fine. I'll pack a suitcase and we'll go to your home. Or you pack a suitcase and come to mine. I am infinitely flexible. I'm just not letting you go.'

'Control freak,' said Nicky blissfully.

Esteban was hurrying into his own clothes. He looked up at that, his expression unexpectedly sober. 'Not any more. This last week has taught me that. I can't afford control if I want to hang on to you.'

Nicky was moved. She went up to him, buttoning his shirt like a long-married wife.

'How did you work that out?'

He grimaced. 'With the help of my father, in the end.'

'I thought you didn't talk to him.'

'I didn't. But he came here and saw the state I was in. He gave me some excellent advice—along the lines of not doing everything that he did, admittedly—and persuaded me that I had to stay here and sort things out with you, not go off to New Zealand. So I sent off the work I'd done on the case to the local man and bowed out.'

Nicky was conscience-stricken. 'But the money you were going to earn—you said Hallam needed it.'

Esteban put his arms round her and held her against his chest.

'Felipe again. He has always offered to help but I was too proud. He convinced me that there were things more important than pride.'

Nicky rubbed her face against his shirt-front. 'So why didn't you come to me?'

'I was going to. I was planning it very carefully.'

Nicky was bewildered. 'Planning?'

'There were,' Esteban pointed out drily, 'one or two impediments. Francesca needed a smart reminder of what would happen if she tried any more of her tricks. I couldn't expose you to her malice before I'd got that sorted out.'

'Oh,' said Nicky. She had wondered about Francesca Moran.

'And then there was the glamorous intruder. You said you were not involved with anyone. But you were clearly intimate.' The dark eyes looked fierce for a moment. 'I could have killed him when he said he was your private life.'

Nicky shivered, remembering. 'You said that.'

'He didn't have to agree.'

'He was trying to protect me.'

Esteban said something rude under his breath. 'I knew I was going to have to clear him out of the path one way or another. So I rang the police a couple of days ago and said that I knew him and he'd done it for a bet.'

Nicky was impressed. 'Didn't they charge you with wasting police time?'

'I'm a local employer,' Esteban said cynically. 'All it cost me was a lecture on my irresponsible friends and several tickets to the Police Ball.' He chuckled suddenly. 'In fact that was going to be my excuse to ring you up. I thought I would point out that you got me into it, so it was your moral duty to come with me to the blasted ball.'

'When?' demanded Nicky.

Esteban was startled. 'I don't know. Before Christmas some time. That's when it usually is.'

'I mean when were you going to phone me up?' said Nicky impatiently.

'Not phone. Stand on your doorstep. Tonight. With my heart on my sleeve and a mega helping of humble pie in the shape of two dozen roses,' Esteban said drily.

Nicky choked. 'What?'

'I told you, I've been taking advice from my father,' he said. The amusement was back in his voice. 'He has a rather Latin attitude to these things.'

'Why not until tonight?'

'Because I didn't manage to persuade de Vries to give me your address until today. Apparently your colleagues finally convinced him that you were eating your heart out for me,' he added complacently.

'Eating my—' Nicky was indignant. She strode about the room, mock affronted. 'It's a foul lie. How can you—?'

Her attention was caught by the judge's portrait. She blinked. So that was where the missing tights went. Nicky began to laugh.

Esteban had been settling down for an enjoyable battle. Now he raised one eyebrow. 'What?'

She grinned, pointing. 'For a couple of control freaks, we lost it pretty comprehensively this evening, don't you think?'

Esteban turned, following her finger. He took in the judge's new adornment. His shoulders shook.

'Would you say lost it?' he drawled. 'I'd say we reached new heights.'

He extended a long arm and tugged at the tights. There was a moment of resistance. Then they fell, clearly laddered beyond repair, and the portrait lurched sideways. It was too much. Nicky let out a delighted peal of laughter and clung to Esteban.

He looked down at her, his mouth curling wickedly.

'I can see you're going to be a terrible influence,' he murmured.

Nicky looked up at him. There was so much love in his eyes, he was almost unrecognisable. Her laughter quietened.

'I hope so,' she whispered. 'I do hope so.'

The wicked mouth was fierce on hers.

'Count on it,' said Esteban.

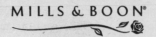

MILLS & BOON®

Makes
any time
special

Enjoy a romantic novel from
Mills & Boon®

Presents...™   *Enchanted*™   TEMPTATION.

Historical Romance™   ✛MEDICAL ROMANCE™

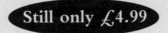

COMING NEXT MONTH

MILLS & BOON®

Enchanted™

THE NINE-MONTH BRIDE by Judy Christenberry

Susannah longed for a baby and Lucas desperately wanted a son, but not the emotional ties of marriage. So they decided to make a convenient marriage, then make a baby – the old-fashioned way…

THE BOSS AND THE BEAUTY by Donna Clayton

Cindy was determined to make her boss, Kyle, see her as a woman rather than his employee. But as Kyle *never* mixed business with pleasure—it was going to be a long haul to get this man from the boardroom to the altar!

TAMING JASON by Lucy Gordon

Jason was injured and temporarily blind, and for his sake Elinor must keep her identity a secret. What would happen when he was able to see her again – and recognise her as the woman he'd once considered unsuitable for marriage?

A HUSBAND WORTH WAITING FOR
by Grace Green

After his accident Jed's memory loss turned him into an entirely different man. Sarah found him charming—even seductive! But how long until Jed's memory returned? And when it did, would he still be a husband worth waiting for?

Available from 4th February 2000

COMING NEXT MONTH

MILLS & BOON®

Enchanted™

BORROWED BACHELOR by Barbara Hannay

Maddy needed a man who'd pretend to be her boyfriend, and her sexy neighbour Rick seemed ideal. Yet Rick played the part of the attentive lover so convincingly that even Maddy's mind turned towards marriage…

MEANT FOR YOU by Patricia Knoll

Jed thinks Caitlin is too uptight. She thinks Jed is too laid-back. All they have to do is stick to their separate sides of the house. So why do they keep meeting in the hallway?

MARRYING MARGOT by Barbara McMahon

The worst time in Rand's life had been when he and Margot had lost their baby and their young marriage had floundered. Now Rand wanted a reconciliation and more children. Margot still loved him, but she couldn't go through the heartache again…

THE BILLIONAIRE DADDY by Renee Roszel

Baby Tina needed a mum and her aunt Lauren wanted to take on the role—as soon as she had dealt with Tina's so-called 'father', Dade Delacourt. When Dade mistook Lauren for Tina's nanny the mistake gave Lauren the ideal opportunity to check out Dade's parenting skills. Except the plan backfired because the irresistible billionaire expected her to be with him twenty-four hours a day…

Available from 4th February 2000

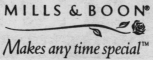

2 FREE

books and a surprise gift!

We would like to take this opportunity to thank you for reading this Mills & Boon® book by offering you the chance to take TWO more specially selected titles from the Enchanted™ series absolutely FREE! We're also making this offer to introduce you to the benefits of the Reader Service™—

- ★ FREE home delivery
- ★ FREE gifts and competitions
- ★ FREE monthly Newsletter
- ★ Exclusive Reader Service discounts
- ★ Books available before they're in the shops

Accepting these FREE books and gift places you under no obligation to buy, you may cancel at any time, even after receiving your free shipment. Simply complete your details below and return the entire page to the address below. *You don't even need a stamp!*

YES! Please send me 2 free Enchanted books and a surprise gift. I understand that unless you hear from me, I will receive 4 superb new titles every month for just £2.40 each, postage and packing free. I am under no obligation to purchase any books and may cancel my subscription at any time. The free books and gift will be mine to keep in any case.

N0EA

Ms/Mrs/Miss/Mr ....Initials.....................................
                                                    BLOCK CAPITALS PLEASE

Surname ....

Address ....

....

....Postcode...................................

Send this whole page to:
UK: FREEPOST CN81, Croydon, CR9 3WZ
EIRE: PO Box 4546, Kilcock, County Kildare (stamp required)